Goosebumps TV Special

1

The Cuckoo Clock of Doom

The Girl Who Cried Monster

Other TV Specials available:

2: Welcome to Camp Nightmare
   Piano Lessons Can Be Murder

3: Return of the Mummy
   Phantom of the Auditorium

And look out for:

4: Night of the Living Dummy II
   Say Cheese and Die!

5: It Came From Beneath the Sink
   My Hairiest Adventure

1

The Cuckoo Clock of Doom

The Girl Who Cried Monster

R.L. Stine

Hippo

Scholastic Children's Books,
Commonwealth House, 1–19 New Oxford Street, London WC1A lNU, UK
a division of Scholastic Ltd
London ~ New York ~ Toronto ~ Sydney ~ Auckland

First published in this edition by Scholastic Ltd, 1997

The Cuckoo Clock of Doom
First published in the USA by Scholastic Inc., 1995
First published in the UK by Scholastic Ltd, 1996
Copyright © Parachute Press, Inc., 1995
The Girl Who Cried Monster
First published in the USA by Scholastic Inc., 1993
First published in the UK by Scholastic Ltd, 1994
Copyright © Parachute Press, Inc., 1993

GOOSEBUMPS is a trademark of Parachute Press, Inc.

ISBN 0 590 19864 5
All rights reserved

Typeset by Contour Typesetters, Southall, London
Printed by Cox & Wyman Ltd, Reading, Berks

10 9 8 7 6 5 4 3 2 1

CONTENTS

The Cuckoo Clock
of Doom

"Michael, your shoe's untied."

My sister, Tara, sat on the front steps, grinning at me. Another one of her dumb jokes.

I'm not an idiot. I knew better than to look down at my shoe. If I did, she'd slap me under the chin or something.

"I'm not falling for that old trick," I told her.

Mum had just called me and the brat inside for dinner. An hour before she had made us go outside because she couldn't stand our fighting any more.

It was impossible not to fight with Tara.

When it comes to stupid tricks, Tara never knows when to quit. "I'm not kidding," she insisted. "Your shoe's untied. You're going to trip."

"Knock it off, Tara," I said. I started up the front steps.

My left shoe seemed to cling to the cement. I pulled it up with a jerk.

3

"Yuck!" I'd stepped on something sticky.

I glanced at Tara. She's a skinny little squirt, with a wide red mouth like a clown's and stringy brown hair that she wears in two pigtails.

Everyone says she looks exactly like me. I hate it when they say that. My brown hair is not stringy, for one thing. It's short and thick. And my mouth is normal-sized. No one has ever said I look like a clown.

I'm a little short for my age, but not skinny.

I do *not* look like Tara.

She was watching me, giggling. "You'd better look down," she taunted in her singsong voice.

I glanced down at my shoe. It wasn't untied, of course. But I'd just stepped on a huge wad of gum. If I had looked down to check my shoelaces, I would have seen it.

But Tara knew I *wouldn't* look down. Not if she told me to.

Tricked by Tara the Terror again.

"You're going to get it, Tara," I grumbled. I tried to grab her, but she dodged out of reach and ran into the house.

I chased her into the kitchen. She screamed and hid behind my mother.

"Mum! Hide me! Michael's going to get me!" she shrieked.

As if she were afraid of me. Fat chance.

"Michael Webster!" Mum scolded. "Stop chasing your little sister."

4

She glanced at my feet and added, "Is that gum on your shoe? Oh, Michael, you're tracking it all over the floor!"

"Tara *made* me step on it!" I whined.

Mum frowned. "Do you expect me to believe that? Michael, you're fibbing again."

"I am not!" I cried.

Mum shook her head in disgust. "If you're going to tell a lie, Michael, at least make it a good one."

Tara peeked out from behind Mum and taunted me. "Yeah, *Michael.*"

Then she laughed. She loved this.

She's always getting me into trouble. My parents always blame me for stuff that's *her* fault. But does Tara ever do anything wrong? Oh, *no*, never. She's a perfect angel. Not a bad bone in her body.

I'm twelve. Tara's seven. She's made the last seven years of my life miserable.

Too bad I don't remember the first five very well. The pre-Tara years. They must have been awesome! Quiet and peaceful—and fun!

I went out to the back porch and scraped the sticky gum off my shoe. I heard the doorbell ring and Dad calling, "It's here! I'll get it."

Inside, everybody gathered around the front door. Two men were struggling to carry something heavy into the house. Something long and narrow and wrapped with padded grey cloth.

"Careful," Dad warned them. "It's very old. Bring it in here."

Dad let the delivery guys into the den. They set the thing down on one end and began to unwrap it. It was about as wide as me and maybe thirty centimetres taller.

"What is it?" Tara asked.

Dad didn't answer right away. He rubbed his hands together in anticipation. Our cat, Bubba, slinked into the room and rubbed against Dad's legs.

The grey cloth fell away, and I saw a very fancy old clock. It was mostly black but painted with lots of silver, gold and blue designs, and decorated with scrolls, carvings, knobs and buttons.

The clock itself had a white face with gold hands and gold Roman numerals. I saw little secret doors hidden under the paint designs, and a big door in the middle of the clock.

The delivery guys gathered up the grey padding. Dad gave them some money, and they left.

"Isn't it great?" Dad gushed. "It's an antique cuckoo clock. It was a bargain. You know that shop opposite my office, Anthony's Antiques and Stuff?"

We all nodded.

"It's been in the shop for fifteen years," Dad told us, patting the clock. "Every time I pass

Anthony's, I stop and stare at it. I've always loved it. Anthony finally put it on sale."

"Cool," Tara said.

"But you've been bargaining with Anthony for years, and he always refused to lower the price," Mum said. "Why now?"

Dad's face lit up. "Well, today I went into the shop at lunchtime, and Anthony told me he'd discovered a tiny flaw on the clock. Something wrong with it."

I scanned the clock. "Where?"

"He wouldn't say. Do you see anything, kids?"

Tara and I began to search the clock for flaws. All the numbers on the face were correct, and both the hands were in place. I didn't see any chips or scratches.

"I don't see anything wrong with it," Tara said.

"Me, neither," I added.

"Neither do I," Dad agreed. "I don't know what Anthony's talking about. I told him I wanted to buy the clock anyway. He tried to talk me out of it, but I insisted. If the flaw is so tiny we don't even notice it, what difference does it make? Anyway, I really do love this thing."

Mum cleared her throat. "I don't know, dear. Do you think it really belongs in the den?" I could tell by her face that she didn't like the clock as much as Dad did.

"Where else could we put it?" Dad asked.

"Well—maybe the garage?"

Dad laughed. "I get it—you're joking!"

Mum shook her head. She wasn't joking. But she didn't say anything more.

"I think this clock is just what the den needs, honey," Dad added.

On the right side of the clock I saw a little dial. It had a gold face and looked like a miniature clock. But it had only one hand.

Tiny numbers were painted in black along the outside of the dial, starting at 1800 and ending at 2000. The thin gold hand pointed to one of the numbers: 1995.

The hand didn't move. Beneath the dial, a little gold button had been set into the wood.

"Don't touch that button, Michael," Dad warned. "This dial tells the current year. The button moves the hand to change the year."

"That's kind of silly," Mum said. "Who ever forgets what year it is?"

Dad ignored her. "See, the clock was built in 1800, where the dial starts. Every year the pointer moves one notch to show the date."

"So why does it stop at two thousand?" Tara asked.

Dad shrugged. "I don't know. I guess the clockmaker couldn't imagine the year two thousand would ever come. Or maybe he figured the clock wouldn't last that long."

"Maybe he thought the world would blow up in 1999," I suggested.

"Could be," Dad said. "Anyway, please don't touch the dial. In fact, I don't want anyone touching the clock at all. It's very old and very, very delicate. Okay?"

"Okay, Dad," Tara said.

"I won't touch it," I promised.

"Look," Mum said, pointing at the clock. "It's six o'clock. Dinner's almost—"

Mum was interrupted by a loud gong. A little door just over the clock face slid open—and a bird flew out. It had the meanest bird face I ever saw—and it dived for my head.

I screamed. "It's alive!"

Cuckoo! Cuckoo!

The bird flapped its yellow feathers. Its eerie, bright blue eyes glared at me. It squawked six times. Then it jumped back inside the clock. The little door slid shut.

"It's not alive, Michael," Dad said, laughing. "It sure is real-looking, though, isn't it? Wow!"

"You birdbrain!" Tara teased. "You were scared! Scared of a cuckoo clock!" She reached out and pinched me.

"Get off me," I growled. I shoved her away.

"Michael, don't push your sister," Mum said. "You don't realize how strong you are. You could hurt her."

"Yeah, Michael," Tara said.

Dad kept admiring the clock. He could hardly take his eyes off it. "I'm not surprised the cuckoo startled you," he said. "There's something special about this clock. It comes from the

10

Black Forest of Germany. It's supposed to be enchanted."

"Enchanted?" I echoed. "You mean, magic? How?"

"Legend has it that the man who built this clock had magical powers. He put a spell on the clock. They say if you know the secret, you can use the clock to go back in time."

Mum scoffed. "Did Anthony tell you that? What a great way to sell an old clock. Claim it has magic powers!"

Dad wouldn't let her spoil his fun. "You never know," he said. "It could be true. Why not?"

"I think it's true," Tara said.

"Herman, I wish you wouldn't tell the kids these wild stories," Mum chided. "It's not good for them. And it only encourages Michael. He's always making things up, telling fibs and impossible stories. I think he gets it from you."

I protested. "I don't make things up! I *always* tell the truth!"

How could Mum say that about me?

"I don't think it hurts the kids to use their imaginations once in a while," Dad said.

"Imagination is one thing," Mum said. "Lies and fibs are something else."

I fumed. Mum was so unfair to me. The worst part was the expression of victory on Tara's face. Making me look bad was her mission in life. I wanted to wipe that smirk off her face for ever.

"Dinner's almost ready," Mum announced, leaving the den. The cat followed her. "Michael, Tara—go and wash your hands."

"And remember," Dad warned. "No one touches the clock."

"Okay, Dad," I said.

Dinner smelled good. I started for the bathroom to wash. As I passed Tara, she stomped hard on my foot.

"Ow!" I yelled.

"Michael!" Dad barked. "Stop making so much noise."

"But, Dad, Tara stomped on my foot."

"It couldn't have hurt that much, Michael. She's a lot smaller than you are."

My foot throbbed. I limped to the bathroom. Tara followed me.

"You're such a baby," she taunted.

"Be quiet, Tara," I said. How did I get the worst sister in the world?

We had pasta with broccoli and tomato sauce for dinner. Mum was on a big no-meat, low-fat kick. I didn't mind. Pasta was better than what we'd had the night before—lentil soup.

"You know, honey," Dad complained to Mum, "a hamburger now and then never hurt anybody."

"I disagree," Mum said. She didn't have to say more. We'd all heard her lectures about meat and fat and chemicals before.

Dad covered his pasta with a thick layer of Parmesan cheese.

"Maybe the den should be off limits for a while," Dad suggested. "I hate to think of you two playing in there and breaking the clock."

"But, Dad, I have to do my homework in the den tonight," I said. "I'm doing a report on 'Transportation in Many Lands'. And I need to use the encyclopaedia."

"Can't you take it up to your room?" Dad asked.

"The whole encyclopaedia?"

Dad sighed. "No, I guess you can't. Well, all right. You can use the den tonight."

"I need to use the encyclopaedia, too," Tara announced.

"You do not," I snapped. She wanted to hang around the den and bug me, that was all.

"I do, too. I'm supposed to read about the gold rush."

"You're making that up. You don't study the gold rush in the second grade. That's not until fourth."

"What do you know about it? Mrs Dolin is teaching us the gold rush *now*. Maybe I'm in a smarter class than you were."

13

Mum said, "Michael, really. If Tara says she needs to use the encyclopaedia, why start a fight about it?"

I sighed and stuffed a forkful of pasta in my mouth. Tara stuck her tongue out at me.

There's no point in talking, I thought. All it does is get me into trouble.

I lugged my backpack into the den after dinner. No sign of Tara—yet. Maybe I'd be able to get some homework done before she came in and started pestering me.

I dumped my books on Dad's desk. The clock caught my eye. It wasn't pretty—kind of ugly, really. But I liked looking at all those scrolls and buttons and knobs. It really did seem as if the clock could be magic.

I thought about the flaw Dad had mentioned. I wondered what it was. Some kind of bump? A missing notch on one of the gears? Maybe a piece of chipped paint?

I glanced back at the door to the den. Bubba wandered through it, purring. I petted him.

Mum and Dad were still in the kitchen, cleaning up after dinner. I didn't think it would matter if I just looked at the clock a little.

Careful not to touch any buttons, I stared at the dial that showed the year. I ran my fingers along a curve of silver at the edge of the clock. I glanced at the little door over the face of the clock. I knew the cuckoo sat behind the door, waiting to leap out at the right time.

I didn't want to be surprised by the bird again. I checked the time. Five minutes to eight.

Under the face of the clock I saw another door. A big door. I touched its gold knob.

What's behind this door? I wondered. Maybe the gears of the clock, or a pendulum.

I glanced over my shoulder again. No one was looking. No problem if I just peeked behind that big clock door.

I tugged on the gold knob. The door was stuck. I pulled harder.

The door flew open.

I let out a scream as an ugly green monster burst out of the clock. It grabbed me and knocked me to the floor.

"Mum! Dad! Help!" I shrieked.

The monster raised its long claws over me. I covered my face, waiting to be slashed.

"Goochy goochy goo!" The monster giggled and tickled me with its claws.

I opened my eyes. Tara! Tara in her old Halloween costume!

She rolled on the floor, giggling. "You're so easy to scare!" she shouted. "You should have seen your face when I jumped out of the clock!"

"It's not funny!" I cried. "It's—"

Gong.

Cuckoo, cuckoo, cuckoo, cuckoo!

The bird popped out of the clock and started cuckoo-ing. Okay, I admit it scared me again. But did Tara have to clutch her sides, laughing at me that way?

"What's going on in here?" Dad stood in the doorway, glaring down at us.

16

He pointed at the clock. "What's that door doing open? Michael, I *told* you to stay away from the clock!"

"ME?" I cried.

"He was trying to catch the cuckoo," Tara lied.

"I *thought* so," Dad said.

"Dad, that's not true! Tara's the one who—"

"Enough of that, Michael. I'm sick of hearing you blame Tara every time you do something wrong. Maybe your mother is right. Maybe I have been encouraging your imagination a little too much."

"That's not fair!" I yelled. "I don't have any imagination! I *never* make anything up!"

"Dad, he's lying," Tara said. "I came in here and saw him playing with the clock. I tried to stop him."

Dad nodded, swallowing every word his precious Tara said.

There was nothing I could do. I stormed off to my room and slammed the door.

Tara was the biggest pain in the world, and she never got blamed for anything. She even ruined my birthday.

I turned twelve three days ago. Usually, people like their birthday. It's supposed to be fun, right?

Not for me. Tara made sure my birthday was

17

the worst day of my life. Or at least *one* of the worst.

First, she ruined my present.

I could tell my parents were very excited about this present. My mother kept hopping around like a chicken, saying, "Don't go in the garage, Michael! Whatever you do, don't go in the garage!"

I knew she'd hidden my present in there. But just to torture her, I asked, "Why not? Why can't I go in the garage? The lock on my bedroom door is broken, and I need to borrow one of Dad's tools..."

"No, no!" Mum exclaimed. "Tell your father to fix the lock. He'll get the tools. You can't go in there, because... well... there's a huge mound of rubbish in there. It really stinks. It smells so bad, you could get sick from it!"

Sad, isn't it? And she thinks I get my "imagination" from Dad!

"All right, Mum," I promised. "I won't go in the garage."

And I didn't—even though the lock on my door really was broken. I didn't want to spoil whatever surprise they had cooked up.

They were throwing me a big birthday party that afternoon. A bunch of kids from school were coming over. Mum baked a cake and made snacks for the party. Dad ran around the house, setting up chairs and hanging crêpe paper.

18

"Dad, would you mind fixing the lock on my door?" I asked.

I like my privacy—and I *need* that lock. Tara had broken it a week earlier. She'd been trying to kickbox the door down.

"Sure, Michael," Dad agreed. "Anything you say. After all, you're the birthday boy."

"Thanks."

Dad took the toolbox upstairs and worked on the lock. Tara lounged around the dining room making trouble. As soon as Dad was gone, she pulled down a crêpe paper streamer and left it lying on the floor.

Dad fixed the lock and returned the tools to the garage. As he passed through the dining room, he noticed the torn-down streamer.

"Why won't this crêpe paper stay up?" he mumbled. He taped it back up. A few minutes later, Tara tore it down again.

"I know what you're doing, Tara," I told her. "Stop trying to wreck my birthday."

"I don't have to wreck it," she said. "It's bad all by itself—just because it's the day you were born." She pretended to shudder in horror.

I ignored her. It was my birthday. Nothing could keep me from having fun, not even Tara.

That's what I *thought*.

About half an hour before the party, Mum and Dad called me into the garage.

I pretended to go along with Mum's silly story. "What about the horrible rubbish?"

"Oh, that," Mum clucked. "I made it up."

"Really?" I said. "Wow. It was so believable."

"If you believed that, you must be a moron," Tara said.

Dad threw open the garage door. I stepped inside.

There stood a brand-new 21-speed bike. The bike I'd wanted for a long time.

The coolest bike I'd ever seen!

"Do you like it?" Mum asked.

"I love it!" I cried. "It's awesome! Thanks!"

"Cool bike, Mike," Tara said. "Mum, I want one of these for *my* birthday."

Before I could stop her, she climbed up on the seat of my new bike.

"Tara, get off!" I yelled.

She didn't listen. She tried to reach her feet to the pedals, but her legs were too short. The bike fell over.

"Tara!" Mum cried, running to the little brat's side. "Are you hurt?"

Tara stood up and brushed herself off. "I'm okay. I scraped my knee a little, though."

I picked up my bike and inspected it. It was no longer perfectly shiny and black. There was a huge white scratch across the middle bar.

It was practically ruined.

"Tara, you wrecked my bike!"

"Let's not get overexcited, Michael," Dad said. "It's only a scratch."

"Don't you even care about your sister?" Mum asked. "She could've been hurt!"

"It's her own fault! She shouldn't have touched my bike in the first place!"

"Michael, you have a lot to learn about being a good brother," Dad said.

They make me so mad sometimes!

"Let's go inside," Mum said. "Your friends will be here soon."

The party. I thought the party would make me feel better. After all, there would be cake, presents, and my best friends. What could go wrong?

It started out okay. One by one my friends arrived, and they all brought me presents. I'd invited five guys: David, Josh, Michael B., Henry and Lars; and three girls: Ceecee, Rosie and Mona.

I wasn't so crazy about Ceecee and Rosie, but I really liked Mona. She has long, shiny brown hair and a turned-up nose that's kind of cute. She's tall, and good at basketball. There's something sort of cool about her.

Ceecee and Rosie are Mona's best friends. I had to invite them if I was going to invite Mona. They always go everywhere together.

Ceecee, Rosie and Mona arrived all at once.

They took off their jackets. Mona was wearing pink dungarees over a white turtleneck. She looked great. I didn't care what the other girls were wearing.

"Happy birthday, Michael!" they all called out at the door.

"Thanks," I said.

They each handed me a gift. Mona's was small and flat and wrapped in silver paper. Probably a CD, I figured. But which one? What kind of CD would a girl like Mona think a guy like me would like?

I set the presents on top of the pile in the living room.

"Hey, Michael—what did your parents give you?" David asked.

"Just a bike," I said, trying to be cool about it. "A twenty-one speed."

I put on a CD. Mum and Tara brought in plates of sandwiches. Mum went back to the kitchen, but Tara stayed.

"Your little sister is so cute," Mona said.

"Not once you get to know her," I muttered.

"Michael! That's not very nice," Mona said.

"He's a terrible big brother," Tara told her. "He yells at me all the time."

"I do not! Get lost, Tara."

"I don't have to." She stuck her tongue out at me.

22

"Let her stay, Michael," Mona said. "She's not bothering anybody."

"Hey, Mona," Tara chirped. "You know, Michael really likes you."

Mona's eyes widened. "He does?"

My face got red-hot. I glared at Tara. I wanted to strangle her right then and there. But I couldn't—too many witnesses.

Mona started laughing. Ceecee and Rosie laughed, too. Luckily, the guys didn't hear this. They were around the CD player, skipping from cut to cut.

What could I say? I *did* like Mona. I couldn't deny it—it would hurt her feelings. But I couldn't admit it, either.

I wanted to die. I wanted to sink through the floor and die.

"Michael, your face is all red!" Mona cried.

Lars heard this and called out, "What did Webster do now?"

Some of the guys call me by my last name.

I grabbed Tara and dragged her into the kitchen, Mona's laughter ringing in my ears.

"Thanks a lot, Tara," I whispered. "Why did you have to tell Mona I like her?"

"It's true, isn't it?" the brat said. "I always tell the truth."

"Yeah, right!"

"Michael—" Mum interrupted. "Are you being mean to Tara again?"

I stormed out of the kitchen without answering her.

"Hey, Webster," Josh called when I returned to the living room. "Let's see your new bike."

Good, I thought. A way to get away from the girls.

I led them to the garage. They all stared at the bike and nodded at each other. They seemed really impressed. Then Henry grabbed the handlebars.

"Hey, what's this big scratch?" he said.

"I know," I explained. "My sister . . ."

I stopped and shook my head. What was the use?

"Let's go back and open my presents," I suggested.

We trooped back into the living room.

At least I've got more presents coming, I thought. Tara can't ruin those.

But Tara always find a way.

When I entered the living room, I found Tara sitting in the middle of a pile of torn-up wrapping paper. Rosie, Mona and Ceecee sat around her, watching.

Tara had opened all my presents for me.

Thanks so much, Tara.

She was ripping open the last present—Mona's.

"Look what Mona gave you, Michael!" Tara shouted.

It *was* a CD.

"I've heard there are some great *love* songs on it," Tara teased.

Everybody laughed. They all thought Tara was a riot.

Later, we all sat down in the dining room for cake and ice-cream. I carried the cake myself. Mum followed me, holding plates, candles, and matches.

It was my favourite kind of cake, chocolate-chocolate.

Balancing the cake in my hands, I stepped through the kitchen door and into the dining room.

I didn't see Tara pressed against the wall. I didn't see her stick her bratty little foot in the doorway.

I tripped. The cake flew out of my hands.

I landed on top of the cake. Face down. Of course.

Some kids gasped. Some tried to muffle their laughter.

I sat up and wiped the brown frosting from my eyes.

The first face I saw was Mona's. She was shaking with laughter.

Mum leaned over and scolded me. "What a mess! Michael, why don't you look where you're going?"

I listened to the laughter and stared at my ruined cake. I had no candles to blow out now. But it didn't matter. I decided to make a wish, anyway.

I wish I could start this birthday all over again.

I stood up, covered in gooey brown cake. My friends howled.

"You look like the Hulk!" Rosie cried.

Everybody laughed harder than ever.

They all had a great time at my party. Everyone did.

Except for me.

My birthday was bad—very bad. But ruining it wasn't the worst thing Tara did to me.

Nobody would believe the worst thing.

It happened the week before my birthday. Mona, Ceecee and Rosie were coming over. We all had parts in the school play, and planned to rehearse together at my house.

The play was a new version of *The Frog Prince*. Mona played the princess, and Ceecee and Rosie were her two silly sisters. Perfect casting, I thought.

I played the frog, before the princess kissed him and turns him into a prince. For some reason, our drama teacher didn't want me to play the prince. Josh got that part.

Anyway, I decided that the frog is a better part. Because Mona, the princess, kisses the *frog*, not the prince.

The girls would arrive any minute.

Tara sat on the rug in the den, torturing our cat, Bubba. Bubba hated Tara almost as much as I did.

Tara lifted Bubba by the hind legs, trying to

make him do a handstand. Bubba yowled and squirmed and wriggled away. But Tara caught him and made him do a handstand again.

"Stop that, Tara," I ordered.

"Why?" Tara said. "It's fun."

"You're hurting Bubba."

"No, I'm not. He likes it. See? He's smiling." She let go of his hind legs and grabbed him with one hand under his front legs. With the other hand she lifted the corners of his mouth and stretched them into a pained smile.

Bubba tried to bite her. He missed.

"Tara," I said, "let him go. And get out of here. My friends are coming over."

"No." Now Tara tried to make Bubba walk on his front paws. He fell and bumped his nose.

"Tara, stop it!" I cried. As I tried to take Bubba away from her, she let the cat go. Bubba meowed and scratched me across the arm.

"Ow!" I dropped Bubba. He ran away.

"Michael, what were you doing to that cat?" Mum stood in the doorway. Bubba slipped past her into the hall.

"Nothing! He scratched me!"

"Stop teasing him, and he won't scratch you," Mum scolded. She left, calling over her shoulder, "I'm going upstairs to lie down for a while. I have a headache."

The doorbell rang. "We'll get it, Mum!" I called.

I knew it must be the girls at the door. I wanted to surprise them in my frog costume, but I wasn't ready yet.

"Answer the door, Tara," I told the brat. "Tell Mona and the others to wait for me in the den. I'll be right back."

"Okay," Tara said. She trotted off to the front door. I hurried upstairs to change into my costume.

I pulled the costume out of my closet. I took off my trousers and shirt. I picked up the frog suit, trying to open the zipper. It was stuck.

I stood there in my underwear, tugging at the zipper. Then my bedroom door clicked open.

"Here he is, girls," I heard Tara say. "He told me to bring you upstairs."

No! I thought. *Please* don't let it be true!

I was afraid to look up. I knew what I'd see.

The door wide open. Mona, Ceecee, Rosie and Tara, staring at me in my underwear!

I forced myself to look. It was worse than I'd thought.

There they all stood—staring and laughing!

Tara laughed hardest of all. She laughed like a rotten little hyena.

You think that's bad? Wait. There's more.

Two days before the underwear disaster, I was

hanging around after school, playing basketball in the gym with Josh, Henry, and some other guys, including Kevin Flowers.

Kevin is a good player, big and tough. He is twice as tall as me! He loves basketball. The Duke Blue Devils are his favourite college team. He wears a Blue Devils cap to school every day.

While we were shooting baskets, I spied Tara hanging around the sidelines, where we'd all tossed our jackets and backpacks against the wall.

I got a bad feeling. I always do when Tara's around.

What's she doing there? I wondered.

Maybe her teacher kept her after school, and she's waiting for me to walk her home.

She's just trying to distract me, I told myself. Don't let her. Don't think about her. Just concentrate on the game.

I felt good. I actually sank a few baskets before the game ended. My side won. We had Kevin Flowers on our team, that's why.

We all jogged to the wall to get our packs. Tara was gone.

Funny, I thought. I guess she went home without me.

I hoisted my pack over my shoulder and said, "See you tomorrow, guys."

But Kevin's voice boomed through the gym. "Nobody move!"

We all froze.

"Where's my cap?" he demanded. "My Blue Devils cap is missing!"

I shrugged. *I* didn't know where his stupid cap was.

"Somebody took my cap," Kevin insisted. "Nobody leaves until we find it."

He grabbed Henry's backpack and started pawing through it. Everyone knows how much Henry loves that cap.

But Josh pointed at me. "Hey—what's that hanging out of Webster's pack?" he asked.

"My pack?" I cried. I glanced over my shoulder.

I saw a patch of blue sticking out of the zippered pocket.

My stomach lurched.

Kevin strode over to me and ripped the cap out of my pack.

"I don't know how it got there, Kevin," I insisted. "I swear—"

Kevin didn't wait to hear my excuses. He never was much of a listener.

I'll spare you the blood and gore. Let's just say my clothes didn't fit too well when Kevin got through taking me apart!

Josh and Henry helped me home. My mum didn't recognize me. My eyes and nose had traded places with my chin.

While I was in the bathroom cleaning myself

up, I caught a glimpse of Tara in the mirror. The bratty grin on her face told me all I needed to know.

"*You!*" I cried. "You put Kevin's cap in my pack! Didn't you!"

Tara just grinned. Yeah. She did it, all right.

"Why?" I demanded. "Why did you do it, Tara?"

Tara shrugged and tried to look innocent. "Was that Kevin's cap?" she said. "I thought it was yours."

"What a lie!" I cried. "I never wear a Duke cap, and you know it! You did that on purpose!"

I was so furious, I couldn't stand to look at her. I slammed the bathroom door in her face.

And of course I got in trouble for slamming the door.

Now you understand what I had to live with.

Now you know why I did the terrible thing that I did.

Anyone in my place would have done the same.

I stayed in my room that night, thinking hard. Plotting a way to get Tara in trouble.

But nothing came to me. At least, nothing good enough.

Then the clock arrived. A few days later, Tara did something that gave me an idea.

Tara couldn't stay away from the cuckoo clock. One afternoon, Dad caught Tara playing with the clock hands. She didn't get into any *real* trouble, of course—not sweet little Tara. But Dad did say, "I've got my eye on you, young lady. No more playing with the clock."

At last! I thought. At last Dad realizes that Tara's not a perfect angel. And at last I've found a way to get her into big trouble.

If something went wrong with the clock, I knew Tara would be blamed for it.

So I decided to make sure something *did* go wrong.

Tara deserved to get into trouble for the

hundreds of terrible things she did to me.

So *what* if just once she gets blamed for something she didn't do? I thought. It's only evening the score a little.

That night, after everybody was asleep, I sneaked downstairs to the den.

It was almost midnight. I crept up to the clock and waited.

One minute to go.

Thirty seconds.

Ten seconds.

Six, five, four, three, two, one . . .

The gong sounded.

Cuckoo! Cuckoo!

The yellow bird popped out. I grabbed it mid-cuckoo. It made short, strangling noises.

I twisted its head around, so it faced backwards. It looked really funny that way.

It finished out its twelve cuckoos, facing the wrong way.

I laughed to myself. When Dad saw it, he'd go *ballistic*!

The cuckoo slid back into its little window, still facing backwards.

This is going to drive Dad insane! I thought wickedly.

He'll be furious at Tara. He'll explode like a volcano!

Finally, Tara will know what it feels like to be blamed for something you didn't do.

I crept back upstairs. Not a sound. No one saw me.

I fell asleep that night a happy guy. There's nothing like revenge.

I slept late the next morning. I couldn't wait to see Dad blow up at Tara. I just hoped I hadn't missed it already.

I hurried downstairs. I checked the den.

The door stood open.

No one there. No sign of trouble yet.

Good, I thought. I haven't missed it.

I made my way into the kitchen, hungry. Mum, Dad and Tara sat around the table, piled with empty breakfast dishes.

As soon as they saw me, their faces lit up.

"Happy birthday!" they cried all at once.

"Very funny," I snapped. I opened a cabinet. "Is there any more cereal left?"

"Cereal!" Mum said. "Don't you want something special, like pancakes?"

I scratched my head. "Well, sure. Pancakes would be great."

This was a little strange. Usually if I woke up late, Mum said I had to get my own breakfast. And why should I want something special, anyway?

Mum mixed a fresh batch of pancake batter. "Don't go in the garage, Michael! Whatever you do, don't go in the garage!" She hopped up and down, all excited. Just as if it were my birthday again.

Weird.

"... there's a huge mound of rubbish in there," Mum was saying. "It really stinks. It smells so bad, you could get sick from it!"

"Mum, what's with the rubbish story?" I asked. "I didn't believe it the first time."

"Just don't go into the garage," she repeated.

Why was she saying this to me? Why was she acting so weird?

Dad excused himself, saying, "I've got a few important chores to do," in a strange, jolly way.

I shrugged and tried to eat my breakfast in peace. But after breakfast I passed through the dining room. Somebody had decorated it with crêpe paper. One strand had been torn down.

Weird. Totally weird.

Dad came into the room, toolbox in hand. He picked up the torn piece of crêpe paper and started to tape it back up again.

"Why won't this crêpe paper stay up?" he asked.

"Dad," I said. "Why are you covering the dining room with crêpe paper?"

Dad smiled. "Because it's your birthday, of course! Every birthday party needs crêpe paper.

Now, I bet you can't wait to see your present, right?"

I stared at him.

What's going on here? I wondered.

Mum and Dad led me to the garage. Tara followed. They all acted as if they were really going to give me a birthday present.

Dad opened the garage door.

There it was. The bike.

It was perfectly shiny and new-looking. No scratches anywhere.

That must be a surprise, I thought. They figured out a way to get rid of the scratch somehow. Or maybe they got me another new bike!

"Do you like it?" Mum asked.

"It's awesome!" I replied.

Tara said, "Cool bike, Mike. Mum, I want one of these for *my* birthday."

Then she jumped up on the seat. The bike fell over on her. When we pulled it up, it had a big scratch on it.

Mum cried, "Tara! Are you hurt?"

I couldn't believe it. What a nightmare!

It was happening all over again. Exactly as it had happened on my birthday.

What's going on?

"What's wrong, Michael?" Dad asked. "Don't you like the bike?"

What could I say? I felt sick. I felt so confused.

Then it dawned on me.

It must have been my wish, I thought.

My birthday wish.

After Tara tripped me and I fell on my cake, I wished I could go back in time and start my birthday all over again.

Somehow my wish came true.

Wow! I thought. This is kind of cool.

"Let's go inside," Mum said. "The party guests will be here soon."

The party?

Oh, no.

Please no!

Do I have to live through that horrible party again?

Yes.

Yes, I had to live through the whole horrible nightmare again.

My friends all showed up, just like the first time.

I heard Tara say the awful words, "Hey, Mona. You know, Michael really likes you."

Mona said, "He does?"

You already knew that, Mona, I thought. Tara told you four days ago.

You were standing in that very same spot. Wearing those same pink dungarees.

Mona, Ceecee and Rosie cracked up.

I panicked. This can't go on, I thought.

My mother came in, carrying a tray of soda. I grabbed her.

"Mum," I begged. "Please take Tara away. Shut her up in her room or something!"

"Michael, why? Your sister wants to have fun, too."

40

"Mum—*please!*"

"Oh, Michael, you're being silly. Be nice to Tara. She won't bother you. She's just a little girl."

Mum left the room, stranding me with Tara and my friends.

She couldn't save me.

No one could.

I showed the guys my new bike. Henry said, "Hey, what's this big scratch?"

When we got back to the living room, there were all my presents, opened by Tara.

"Look what Mona gave you, Michael!" Tara shouted.

I know, I know, I thought. A CD. With great love songs on it.

"I've heard there are some great *love* songs on it," Tara repeated.

Everybody laughed.

It was just as bad as before.

No. Worse. Because I could see it all coming. And I couldn't stop it.

Could I?

"Michael," Mum called. "Come into the kitchen, please. It's time for the birthday cake!"

Here's the test, I thought, dragging myself into the kitchen.

I'll carry in the cake—but this time I won't trip.

I know Tara is going to try and trip me. I won't let her.

I won't make a fool of myself this time.

I don't have to. I don't have to repeat everything the same way.

Do I?

I stood in the kitchen, staring at the cake. I could hear my friends laughing and talking in the dining room. Tara was in there, too.

I knew she was standing just beyond the dining room door, waiting. Waiting to stick out her foot and trip me. Waiting to make me fall on my face and embarrass myself all over again.

Not this time.

I carefully picked up the cake in both hands. I started towards the dining room.

Mum followed, just as before.

I stopped in front of the entrance to the dining room. I glanced down.

No sign of Tara's foot.

Carefully, watching closely, I stepped through the door. One step.

So far, so good.

Another step. I stood inside the dining room now.

I'd made it! All I had to do was get to the table, about five steps away, and I'd be safe.

I took another step forward. Another.

Then I felt a tug on my foot.

Tara reached out from under the table.

So that was where she'd been hiding. I knew it now. But it was too late.

Everything seemed to move in slow motion. Like in a dream.

I heard an evil giggle.

She grabbed my foot.

Oh, no, I thought. It's happened.

I lost my balance.

As I fell, I turned my head and glanced back.

Tara sat under that table, smirking at me.

I wanted to kill her.

But first I had to fall on my face on a cake.

The cake flew out of my arms. I turned my head again.

Splat!

Everybody gasped with laughter. I sat up and wiped the frosting from my eyes.

Mona leaned over the table, laughing harder than anybody.

The second time was more embarrassing than the first.

I sat on the floor, my face covered with cake, thinking, how could I have been so stupid?

Why did I have to make that wish?

I'll never wish for anything ever again.

I cleaned myself up and managed to survive the rest of the party. When I went to bed that night, I thought, at least it's over.

I switched off the light and pulled the covers up high.

It's over, I repeated. I'll go to sleep, and everything will be back to normal in the morning.

I shut my eyes and fell asleep. But in my dreams, all night long, I saw scenes from my horrible birthday party. The nightmare party became a real nightmare.

There was Tara, telling Mona that I liked her. Mona's face loomed up large in my dreams, laughing, laughing. Ceecee and Rosie and the guys, all laughing right in my face.

I tripped and fell on top of the cake, over and over again.

I tossed and turned. Each dream was scarier than the last. Soon my friends looked like horrible monsters. And Tara was the most horrible of all. Her features melted into a blur as she laughed and laughed at me.

Wake up, I told myself. Wake up!

I dragged myself out of the nightmare world. I sat up in bed, in a cold sweat.

The room was still dark. I glanced at the clock.

Three o'clock in the morning.

I can't sleep, I thought miserably. I can't calm down.

I've got to tell Mum and Dad what happened. Maybe they can help.

Maybe they can make me feel better.

I climbed out of bed and hurried down the dark hall to their room. Their door was open a crack.

I pushed it open.

"Mum? Dad? Are you awake?"

Dad rolled over and grunted, "Huh?"

I shook Mum's shoulder. "Mum?"

Mum stirred. "What is it, Michael?" she whispered. She sat up and grabbed the clock radio. In the clock's dim blue glow I saw her squint, trying to read the time.

"It's three o'clock!" she cried.

Dad snorted and sat up suddenly. "Huh? What?"

"Mum, you've got to listen to me!" I whispered. "Something creepy happened today. Didn't you notice it?"

"Michael, what is this—"

"My birthday," I explained. "Tara ruined my birthday, and I wished I could have it all over again. I wanted to make it better. But I never thought the wish would come true! Then, today, it was my birthday again! And everything happened exactly the same. It was horrible!"

Dad rubbed his eyes. "That you, Michael?"

Mum patted him. "Go back to sleep, dear, Michael's just had a bad dream."

"No, Mum," I cried. "It wasn't a dream. It was real! My birthday happened twice! You were there, both times. Don't you understand?"

"Listen, Michael," Mum began. I heard impatience in her voice. "I know you're excited about your birthday, but it's two days away. Only two days to go—then it will be your birthday at last! Okay? So go back to bed now and get some sleep."

She kissed me good night. "Only two days till your birthday. Sweet dreams."

I staggered back to bed, my head spinning.

Two days until my birthday?

Hadn't I just lived through my birthday—twice?

I switched on the reading lamp and stared at the date on my watch. February third, it said.

My birthday is February fifth. My birthday was two days away.

Could it be true? Was time going backwards?

No, I thought. I must be going nuts.

I shook my head hard. I slapped myself a few times. Going back in time. I laughed at the idea.

It's impossible, I thought. Get a hold of yourself, Michael.

All I did was wish to celebrate my birthday over again—*once*.

I didn't wish to repeat my twelfth birthday

for the rest of my life!

But if that's what's happening, why is it now *two* days before my birthday? Why isn't it just the night before?

Maybe time really *is* going backwards, I thought. Maybe this has nothing to do with my wish.

But, then—why is this happening to me?

I racked my brains.

The clock. Dad's cuckoo clock.

I twisted the cuckoo's head backwards... went to bed . . . and when I woke up, time had gone backwards.

Could that be it? Did *I* do this?

Is Dad's clock really magic?

Maybe I shouldn't have turned that stupid bird backwards, I decided. It figures—I try to get Tara in trouble, and end up getting *myself* into a horrible mess.

Well, if that *is* what happened, it's easy enough to fix.

I'll just go downstairs and turn the cuckoo's head back around.

I tiptoed out of my room and down the stairs. My parents had probably fallen back to sleep already, but I didn't want to take any chances.

I definitely didn't want Dad to catch me fooling around with his precious clock.

My feet hit the cold, bare floor of the hall.

I crept into the den. I switched on a lamp.
 I glanced around the room.
 The cuckoo clock was gone!

"No!" I cried.

Had the clock been stolen?

Without the clock, how could I fix everything? How could I turn the bird's head around and make my life go forward again?

I raced upstairs. I didn't care who I woke up now.

"Mum! Dad!" I yelled. I burst into their room and shook Mum awake again.

"Michael, what is it?" She sounded furious. "It's the middle of the night. We're trying to get some sleep!"

Let them be angry, I thought. This was way more important.

"The cuckoo clock! It's gone!"

Dad rolled over. "What? Huh?"

"Michael, you've had another nightmare," Mum assured me.

"It's not a nightmare, Mum—it's true! Go downstairs and see for yourself! There's no cuckoo clock in the den!"

"Michael—listen to me. It was a dream."
Mum's voice was firm. "We don't own a cuckoo
clock. We never did."

I staggered backwards.

"It's just a dream. A bad dream," she said.

"But Dad bought it . . ."

I stopped.

I understood now.

The date was February third. Two days before
my birthday.

And *five* days before Dad bought the cuckoo
clock.

We were travelling back in time. Dad hadn't
bought the clock yet.

I felt sick.

Mum said, "Michael, are you all right?" She
climbed out of bed and pressed the back of her
hand against my forehead.

"You feel a little warm," she said, nicer
now that she thought I might be sick. "Come
on, let's get you to bed. I'll bet you have a fever—
and that's why you're having all these nightmares."

Dad grunted again. "What? Sick?"

"I'll take care of it, Herman," Mum whispered.
"Go back to sleep."

She guided me back to bed. She thought I was
sick.

But I knew the truth.

I had made time move backwards. And the clock was gone.

How would I fix things now?

By the time I got to the kitchen the next morning, Mum, Dad and Tara had already eaten.

"Hurry up, Michael," Dad said. "You'll be late."

Being late for school didn't seem to matter much at the moment.

"Dad, please sit down for a second," I pleaded. "Just for a minute. It's important."

Dad sat, impatiently, on the edge of a kitchen chair. "Michael, what is it?"

"Mum, are you listening?" I asked.

"Sure, honey," Mum said. She put the milk in the refrigerator and busily wiped off the counter.

"This is going to sound weird," I began. "But I'm not kidding."

I paused. Dad waited. I could tell by the tension in his face he expected me to say something totally dopey.

I didn't disappoint him.

"Dad, time is going backwards. Every day I wake up—and it's an earlier day than the last!"

Dad's face drooped. "Michael, you have a wonderful imagination, but I'm really running

53

late. Can we talk about it when I get home from work tonight? Or why don't you write it down? You know I love reading science fiction stories."

"But, Dad—"

Mum said, "Did somebody remember to feed the cat?"

"*I* did it," Tara said. "Even though it's *supposed* to be *Michael's* job."

"Thanks, Tara," Mum said. "Let's hit the road, everybody."

I grabbed a muffin as Mum hustled us out the door.

They're too busy to understand right now, I reasoned as I hurried to school. Tonight, at dinner, when I have more time to explain . . .

I had lots of time to think about my problem during school. I'd lived through this day before, too. I'd already done all the work, heard all the lessons, eaten the lousy lunch.

When my maths teacher, Mr Parker, turned his back to the class, I knew what would happen next. I predicted it to the second. Kevin Flowers threw an eraser at him and hit him smack on the back of his black trousers.

Now Mr Parker is going to turn around . . . I thought, watching Mr Parker.

He turned around.

. . . now he'll yell at Kevin . . .

Mr Parker shouted, "Kevin Flowers—to the principal's office, now!"

. . . now Kevin will start yelling his head off.

"How do you know it was me!" Kevin yelled. "You didn't see me do anything!"

The rest of the scene happened as I remembered it. Mr Parker cowered a bit—Kevin is pretty big—but told Kevin to go to the principal's office again. Kevin kicked over an empty chair and threw his books across the room.

It was all so boring.

After school, I found Tara in the den, teasing Bubba. She lifted his hind legs and made him walk on his front paws.

"Tara, stop it!" I cried. I tried to take Bubba away from her. She let the cat go. Bubba meowed and scratched me across the arm.

"Ow!" I dropped Bubba. He ran away.

It felt very familiar. And painful.

"Michael, what were you doing to that cat?" Mum demanded.

"Nothing! He scratched me!"

"Stop teasing him, and he won't scratch you," Mum scolded.

The doorbell rang.

Oh, no.

Mona, Ceecee and Rosie. *The Frog Prince.*

The underwear.

I can't let it happen.

But my feet started taking me upstairs. I was walking like a robot to my room.

Why am I doing this? I asked myself.

I'll get my frog costume. The zipper will be stuck.

Tara will open the door, and I'll be standing there in my underpants.

Mona will laugh her head off. I'll want to sink through the floor.

I know all this will happen.

So why am I doing it?

Can't I stop myself?

Don't go upstairs, I begged myself. Don't go to your room.

You don't *have* to do this.

There must be a way to stop it, to control it.

I forced myself to turn around. I walked back down the steps. I sat down on the third step.

Tara answered the door, and soon the girls stood before me in the hall.

Okay, I thought. I'm controlling it. Already things are happening differently from before.

"Michael, where's your costume?" Mona asked. "I really want to see what your costume looks like."

"Uh, no you don't," I said, shrinking a little. "It's really ugly, and I don't want to scare you girls—"

"Don't be a jerk, Michael," Ceecee said. "Why would we be scared by a stupid frog costume?"

"And, anyway, I want to rehearse with it," Mona added. "I don't want to see the costume for the first time on-stage. I'll need to be prepared for it. I need to practise with the costume—and you in it."

"Come on, Michael," Tara put in. "Show them the costume. I want to see it, too."

I flashed her a dirty look. I knew what she had in mind.

"No," I insisted. "I can't do that."

"Why not?" Mona demanded.

"I just can't."

"He's shy!" Rosie exclaimed.

"He's embarrassed," Tara added.

"No, it's not that," I said. "It's just that . . . it's awfully hot in that costume, and—"

Mona leaned close to me. I smelled something sweet, like strawberries. It must've been the shampoo she used. "Come on, Michael," she said. "For me?"

"No."

She stamped her foot. "I won't rehearse our scenes unless you put on that costume!"

I sighed. I didn't see any way out of it.

Mona wouldn't leave me alone until I put on that frog costume.

I gave in. "Okay."

"Hurray!" Tara cried. I gave her another dirty look.

All right, I thought. I may have put on the

costume. But that doesn't mean the girls have to see me in my underwear.

I can still keep that from happening.

I trudged up to my room. But this time, I locked the door.

Now try to embarrass me, Tara, I thought. You can't outsmart Michael Webster. No way.

The door was locked. I felt sure I was safe.

I took off my jeans and my shirt. I dragged the frog costume out of the closet.

I tugged on the zipper. It was stuck.

Just like the last time.

But this time it's okay, I told myself. The door is locked. I have privacy.

Then the door flew open.

I stood helplessly in my underwear. Mona, Rosie and Ceecee stared at me. Then they screamed and started laughing.

"Tara!" I yelled. "The door was locked!"

"No, it wasn't," Tara replied. "The lock's broken, remember?"

"No!" I cried. "Dad fixed it . . . he fixed it . . ."

I tried to remember when Dad had fixed the lock on my bedroom door.

Oh, right.

It was after the underwear nightmare. On my birthday.

So it hadn't happened yet.

How was I supposed to keep all this straight?

Oh, no, I thought. I'm doomed.

Time is all messed up. And I have no way of stopping it.

I began to shake. This was too frightening.

Where would it end? I had no idea. It was getting scarier by the minute.

I could hardly eat dinner that night. I'd eaten it before, of course, and hadn't liked it the first time. Peas, carrots and mushrooms. With brown rice.

I picked at the rice and the carrots. I never eat peas. I slipped them into my napkin when Mum and Dad weren't looking.

I watched Mum, Dad and Tara eat dinner as if nothing were wrong. They sat calmly around the table, saying the same things they'd said last time.

Mum and Dad must notice that something is weird, I thought. They must.

So why don't they say anything about it?

I waited for Dad to finish telling us about his day at work. Then I brought up the subject again. I decided to take it slowly.

"Mum? Dad? Doesn't this dinner seem a little bit familiar?"

"I'll say," Dad replied. "It reminds me of the lunch we ate at that vegetarian restaurant last month. Ugh."

Mum glared at him, then at me. "What are you trying to tell us, Michael?" she said frostily. "Are you tired of eating healthy food?"

"I am," Dad said.

"Me, too," Tara chimed in.

"No. No way," I insisted. "You don't understand. I don't mean that we've eaten food like this before. I mean that we have eaten *this very meal* before. We're eating it twice."

Dad frowned. "No weird theories at the dinner table, please, Michael."

They weren't getting it. I ploughed ahead. "It's not just this dinner. It's this whole day. Haven't you noticed? We're doing everything over! Time is going backwards!"

"Shut up, Michael," Tara said. "This is so boring. Can't we talk about something else?"

"Tara," Mom scolded, "don't say 'shut up'." She turned to me. "Have you been reading those comic books again?"

I grew very frustrated. "You're not listening to me!" I cried. "Tomorrow is going to be yesterday, and the day after that will be the day before! Everything is going backwards!"

Mum and Dad exchanged glances. They seemed to be sharing a secret.

They *do* know something, I thought with excitement. They know something, but they're afraid to tell me.

Mum gazed at me very seriously. "All right, Michael. We might as well tell you," she said. "We're all caught in a time warp, and there's nothing we can do about it."

Mum pushed back her chair. She walked backwards to the stove. She started dishing rice from her plate into the pot on the stove.

"Yenoh, ecir erom?" she asked Dad.

Huh?

"Esaelp, sey," Dad replied.

"Oot, em," Tara said. She spat some rice out on her fork and dumped it back on her plate. She was eating backwards!

Dad stood up and walked backwards to Mum. Then Tara skipped backwards around the kitchen table.

They were all talking and moving backwards. We really *were* in a time warp!

"Hey!" I cried. "It's true!"

Why wasn't I talking backwards, too?

"Norom," Tara said.

She cracked up first. Then Dad started laughing. Then Mum.

I finally caught on. It was a joke. "You—

63

you're all *horrible!*" I cried.

That made them laugh even more.

"I was wondering when you'd figure it out," Tara sneered.

They all sat down at the table again. Mum couldn't help grinning. "We're sorry, Michael. We didn't mean to make fun of you."

"Yes we did!" Tara exclaimed.

I stared at them in horror.

This was the most terrible thing that had ever happened to me. And my parents thought it was a big joke.

Then Dad said, "Michael, did you ever hear of *déjà vu?*"

I shook my head.

"It's when something happens to you and you have the feeling it's happened before," he explained. "Everyone feels that way once in a while. It's nothing to be afraid of."

"Maybe you're nervous about something," Mum added. "Like your birthday coming up. I'll bet you're a little nervous about turning twelve, right? And planning your party and everything?"

"Not really," I protested. "I know that feeling. But this isn't the same thing! This is—"

"Say, Mike," Dad interrupted. "Wait till you see what I got you for your birthday. You're going to flip! It's a big surprise."

No, it isn't, I thought unhappily.

It's not a surprise at all. You've given me that birthday present twice already. How many times are you going to give me that stupid bike?

"Mum, Michael is hiding peas in his napkin again," Tara ratted.

I smushed the peas up in my napkin and threw it in her face.

When I went to school the next morning, I wasn't sure what day it was. It was getting hard to keep track. My classes, my lunch, the stuff my friends said all seemed familiar. But nothing unusual happened. It could have been any day of the school year.

I played basketball after school that day, as usual. While I was playing, a funny feeling crept over me.

A bad feeling.

I've already played this game, I realized. And it didn't end well.

But I kept on playing, waiting to see what would happen.

My team won. We collected our packs.

Then Kevin Flowers yelled, "Where's my Blue Devils cap?"

Oh, yeah, I remembered.

This was *that* basketball game. How could I forget?

Good old Tara. She's done it again!

"Nobody leaves until we find that cap!"

I shut my eyes and handed over my pack.

I knew what was coming. Might as well get it over with.

Getting pounded to a pulp by Kevin Flowers hurt a lot. But at least the pain didn't last long.

The next morning when I woke up, it was all gone. The pain, the scabs, the bruises, everything.

What day is it today? I wondered. It must be a few days before Kevin beat me up.

I hope I won't have to live through that a third time.

But what will happen today?

As I walked to school, I searched for clues. I tried to remember what had happened a day or two before Kevin beat me up.

A maths test? Maybe. I hoped not. But at least it would be easier this time around. I could even try to remember what the problems were and look up all the answers before the test!

I was a little late today. Did that mean something? I wondered. Would I get into trouble?

My form teacher, Ms Jacobson, had closed the classroom door. I opened it. The classroom was already full.

Ms Jacobson didn't look up when I walked in.

I must not be that late, I thought. Guess I won't get in trouble after all.

I started for the back of the room, where I usually sit. As I passed through the rows of desks, I glanced at the other kids.

Who's that guy? I wondered, staring at a chubby, blond kid I'd never seen before.

Then I noticed a pretty girl with cornrows and three earrings in one ear. I'd never seen her before, either.

I stared at all the faces in the classroom. None of the kids looked familiar.

What's going on? I wondered, feeling panic choke my throat.

I don't know *any* of these kids!

Where's my class?

Ms Jacobson finally turned around. She stared at me.

"Hey," the blond kid shouted. "What's a third-grader doing in here?"

Everybody laughed. I couldn't understand why.

A third-grader? Who was he talking about?

I didn't see any third-graders.

"You're in the wrong classroom, young man," Ms Jacobson said to me. She opened the door, showing me the way out.

"I think your room is downstairs on the second floor," she added.

"Thanks," I said. I didn't know what she was talking about. But I decided to go along with her.

She shut the door behind her. I could hear the kids laughing behind the door. I hurried down the hall to the boy's bathroom. I needed to splash some cold water on my face. Maybe that would help.

I turned on the cold water tap. Then I glanced in the mirror, very quickly.

The mirror seems a little higher than usual, I thought.

I washed my hands in the cold water and splashed some on my face.

The sink seems higher, too, I noticed. Strange. Am I in the right school?

I glanced in the mirror again—and got the shock of my life.

Was that *me*?

I looked so *young*.

I ran my head through my short, brushlike brown hair. That dopey crew cut I'd had all through the third grade.

I don't believe it, I thought, shaking my head. I'm a third-grader again!

I've got my third-grade hair. My third-grade clothes. My third-grade body.

But my seventh-grade brain. I think.

Third grade.

That means I've slipped back four years—in one night.

My whole body started to tremble. I grabbed on to the sink to steady myself.

I was suddenly paralysed with fear.

Things were speeding up. Now I'd lost whole years in one night! How old will I be when I wake up tomorrow? I asked myself.

Time was going backward faster and faster—

69

and I still hadn't found a way to stop it!

I shut off the water and dried my face with a paper towel. I didn't know what to do. I was so frightened, I couldn't think straight.

I walked back to my third-grade classroom.

First I glanced through the window of the classroom door. There she was, Mrs Harris, my old third-grade teacher. I'd know that helmet of silver hair anywhere.

And I knew, as soon as I saw her, that I really *had* gone back in time four years.

Because old Mrs Harris shouldn't have been in school that day. She'd retired two years earlier. When I was in fifth grade.

I opened the door and stepped into the classroom.

Mrs Harris didn't bat an eye. "Take a seat, Michael," she commanded. She never mentioned the fact that I was late.

Mrs Harris always liked me.

I checked out the other kids in the class. I saw Henry, Josh, Ceecee and Mona, all little third-graders now.

Mona wore her shiny brown hair in two braids. Ceecee wore hers in one of those stupid side ponytails.

Josh didn't have pimples on his forehead, I noticed. Henry had a sticker on the back of his hand—Donatello, from the Teenage Mutant Hero Turtles.

It was my class all right.

I sat down at an empty desk in the back. My old desk. Right next to Henry.

I glanced at him. He was picking his nose.

Gross. I'd forgotten about that part of being a third-grader.

"Michael, we're on page thirty-three in your spelling book," Mrs Harris informed me.

I reached inside the desk and found my spelling book. I opened it to page thirty-three.

"These are the words you'll need to know for tomorrow's spelling test," Mrs Harris announced. She wrote the words on the board, even though we could read them right there in the spelling book: *Taste, sense, grandmother, easy, happiness*.

"Man," Henry whispered to me. "These words are tough. Look how many letters there are in *grandmother!*"

I didn't know what to say to him. On my last spelling test (when I was still in the seventh grade), I'd had to spell *psychology*. *Grandmother* wasn't a big challenge for me any more.

I zoned out for most of the day. I'd always wished school were easier, but not *this* easy. It was so babyish and boring.

Lunch and break were even worse. Josh chewed up a banana and stuck his tongue out at me. Henry painted his face with chocolate pudding.

71

Finally the school day ended. I dragged my little third-grade body home.

When I opened the front door, I heard a horrible screech. Bubba, just a kitten now, raced past me and out the door. Tara toddled after him.

"Don't tease the cat," I scolded her.

"You're dumb," she replied.

I stared at Tara. She was three years old.

I tried to remember. Had I liked her better when she was three?

"Give me a piggyback!" she cried, tugging on my backpack.

"Get off me," I said.

My pack dropped to the floor. I stooped to pick it up. She grabbed a hunk of my hair and yanked it.

"Ow!" I screamed.

She laughed and laughed.

"That hurt!" I yelled, and shoved her—just as Mum stepped into the hall.

She rushed to Tara's side. "Michael, don't shove your sister. She's only a little girl!"

I stormed off to my room to think.

No, I *hadn't* liked Tara better when she was three. She was as much of a brat as ever.

She was born a brat, and she'd never grow out of it, I knew. She'd be a brat for the rest of her life, driving me crazy even when we're old.

If we ever get to be old, I thought with a

shudder. We'll *never* grow up at this rate.

What am I going to do? I worried. I've slipped back in time four years! If I don't do something fast, I'll be a baby again.

And then what?

A cold shiver ran down my back.

And then what? I asked myself.

Will I disappear *completely*?

I woke up in a panic every morning.

What day was it? What *year* was it?

I had no idea.

I climbed out of bed—it seemed farther away from the floor than it used to—and padded across the hall to the bathroom.

I stared in the mirror. How old was I? Younger than I'd been the day before, I knew that much.

I went back to my room and began to get dressed. Mum had left my clothes for the day folded on a chair in my room.

I examined the jeans I was supposed to wear. They had a picture of a cowboy on the back pocket.

Oh, yeah, I remembered. *These* jeans. The cowboy jeans.

Second grade.

That means I must be seven years old now.

I stepped into the trousers, thinking, I can't believe I have to wear these stupid jeans again.

Then I unfolded the shirt Mum had picked out for me.

My heart sank when I saw it: A cowboy shirt—with fringe and everything.

This is so embarrassing, I thought. How could I have ever let Mum do this to me?

Deep down I knew that I used to like these clothes. I probably picked them out myself.

But I couldn't stand to admit that I'd ever been so stupid.

Downstairs, Tara was still in her pyjamas, watching cartoons. She was now two.

When she saw me pass through the living room, she held out her arms to me. "Kiss! Kiss!" she called.

She wanted me to kiss her? That didn't seem like Tara.

But maybe the two-year-old Tara was still sweet and innocent. Maybe, at two, Tara was actually likeable.

"Kiss! Kiss!" she begged.

"Give poor Tara a kiss," Mum called from the kitchen. "You're her big brother, Michael. She looks up to you."

I sighed. "Okay."

I leaned down to give Tara a kiss on the cheek. With one chubby index finger, she poked me in the eye.

"Ow!" I shrieked.

Tara laughed.

Same old terrible Tara, I thought as I stumbled into the kitchen, one hand over my sore eye.

She was born bad!

This time, at school, I knew which classroom to go to.

There sat all my old friends, Mona and everybody, younger than ever. I'd forgotten how dopey everybody used to look when we were little.

I sat through another dull day of learning stuff I already knew. Subtraction. How to read books with really big print. Perfecting my capital L.

At least it gave me lots of time to think.

Every day I tried to figure out what to do. But I never came up with an answer.

Then I remembered Dad telling us he'd been wanting the cuckoo clock for fifteen years.

Fifteen years! That's it! The clock must be at that antique shop!

I'll go and find the clock, I decided. I couldn't wait for school to end that day.

I figured if I could turn the cuckoo around, time would go forward again. I knew the dial that showed the year must be going backwards, too. All I had to do was reset the date on the clock to the right year, and I'd be twelve again.

I missed being twelve. Seven-year-olds don't

get away with much. Someone's always watching you.

When the school day ended, I started down the block towards my house. I knew the crossing guard was watching me, making sure I'd get home safely.

But at the second block I dashed around the corner to the bus stop. I hoped the crossing guard hadn't seen me.

I stood behind a tree, trying not to be seen.

A few minutes later, a bus pulled over. The doors opened with a hiss. I stepped aboard.

The bus driver eyed me strangely. "Aren't you a little young to be catching the bus by yourself?" he asked me.

"Mind your own business," I replied.

He looked startled, so I added, "I'm meeting Daddy at his office. Mummy said it was okay."

He nodded and let the doors slide shut.

I started to put three quarters in the coin slot, but the driver stopped me after two.

"Whoa, there, buddy," he said, pressing the third quarter into my palm. "Fare's only fifty cents. Keep this quarter for a phone call."

"Oh, yeah. Right." I'd forgotten. They raised the bus fare to 75 cents when I was eleven. But now I was only seven. I put the quarter in my pocket.

The bus pulled away from the kerb and chugged downtown.

I remembered hearing Dad say that Anthony's Antiques and Stuff was across the street from his office. I got off the bus at Dad's block.

I hoped Dad wouldn't see me. I knew I'd be in big trouble if he did.

I wasn't allowed to catch the bus by myself when I was seven.

I hurried past Dad's building and crossed the street. On the corner stood a construction site; just a pile of bricks and rubble, really. Further down the block I saw a black sign with ANTHONY'S ANTIQUES AND STUFF painted on it in gold letters.

My heart began to pound.

I'm almost there, I thought. Soon everything will be all right.

I'll just walk into the shop and find the clock. Then, when no one's looking, I'll turn the cuckoo around and fix the year.

I won't have to worry about waking up tomorrow morning as a three-year-old or something. My life will go back to normal.

Life will seem so easy, I told myself, when time is moving forward the way it's supposed to. Even *with* Tara around!

I gazed through the big plate glass window of the shop. There it stood, right in the window. The clock.

My palms began to sweat, I felt so excited.

I hurried to the shop door and turned the handle.

It wouldn't move. I jiggled it harder.

The door was locked.

Then I noticed a sign, tucked in the bottom corner of the door.

It said, CLOSED FOR VACATION.

I let out a howl of frustration. "NOOO!" I cried. Tears sprang to my eyes. "No! Not after all this."

I banged my head against the door. I couldn't stand it.

Closed for vacation.

How could I have such terrible luck?

How long was Anthony planning to be on vacation? I wondered. How long will the shop be closed?

By the time it reopens, I could be a baby!

I gritted my teeth and thought, there's no way I'm letting that happen. No way!

I've got to do something. *Anything*.

I pressed my nose against the shop window. The cuckoo clock was standing there, a metre or so in front of me.

And I couldn't get to it.

The window stood between me and that clock. The window . . .

Normally, I would never think of doing what I decided to do at that moment.

But I was desperate. I had to reach that clock.

It really was a matter of life and death!

I strolled down the block to the construction site, trying to look casual. Trying not to look like a kid who was planning to break a shop window.

I stuffed my hands in the pockets of my cowboy jeans and whistled. I was sort of grateful to be wearing this stupid cowboy outfit after all. It made me look innocent.

Who would suspect a seven-year-old in a cowboy suit of trying to break into an antique shop?

I kicked around a little dirt at the construction site. Kicked a few rocks. Nobody seemed to be working there.

Slowly I made my way over to a pile of bricks. I glanced around to see if anybody saw me.

The coast was clear.

I picked up a brick and hefted it in my hand. It was very heavy. It wouldn't be easy for me, in my little second-grade body, to throw it far.

But I didn't have to throw it far. Just through the window.

I tried stuffing the brick in my jeans pocket, but it was too big. So I carried it in both hands back to the shop.

81

I tried to look as if it were perfectly normal for a boy to be carrying a brick down the street.

A few adults quickly passed by. No one gave me a second glance.

I stood in front of the shiny plate glass window, weighing the brick in my hand. I wondered if a burglar alarm would go off when I broke the window.

Would I be arrested?

Maybe it wouldn't matter. If I made time to go to the present, I'd escape the police.

Be brave, I told myself. Go for it!

With both hands, I raised the brick over my head . . .

. . . and someone grabbed me from behind.

16

"Help!" I shouted. I spun around. "Dad!"

"Michael, what are you doing here?" Dad demanded. "Are you by yourself?"

I let the brick fall to the pavement. He didn't seem to see it.

"I—I wanted to surprise you," I lied. "I wanted to come and visit you after school."

He stared at me as if he didn't quite understand. So I added, for good measure, "I missed you, Daddy."

He smiled. "You missed me?" He was touched. I could tell.

"How did you get here?" he asked. "On the bus?"

I nodded.

"You know you're not allowed to go on the bus by yourself," he said. But he didn't sound angry. I knew that line about missing him would soften him up.

Meanwhile, I still had the same major

problem—getting my hands on the cuckoo clock.

Could Dad help me? Would he? I was willing to try anything. "Dad," I said, "that clock—"

Dad put his arm around me. "Isn't it a beauty? I've been admiring it for years."

"Dad, I've got to get to the clock," I insisted. "It's very, very important! Do you know when the store will open again? We've got to get that clock somehow!"

Dad misunderstood me. He patted me on the head and said, "I know how you feel, Michael. I wish I could have the clock right now. But I can't afford it. Maybe some day . . ."

He pulled me away from the shop. "Come on— let's go home. I wonder what's for supper tonight?"

I didn't say another word all the way home in the car. All I could think about was the clock— and what would happen to me next.

How old will I be when I wake up tomorrow? I wondered.

Or how young?

When I opened my eyes the next morning, everything had changed.

The walls were painted baby blue. The bedspread and the curtains matched. The material was printed with bouncing kangaroos. On one wall hung a needlepoint picture of a cow.

It wasn't my room, but it looked familiar.

Then I felt a lump in the bed. I reached under the kangaroo covers and pulled out Harold, my old teddy bear.

I slowly understood. I was back in my old bedroom.

How had I ended up there? It was Tara's room now.

I jumped out of bed. I was wearing smurf pyjamas.

I swear I don't remember ever liking smurfs that much.

I ran to the bathroom to look in the mirror.

How old was I now?

I couldn't tell. I had to stand on the toilet seat to see my face.

A bad sign.

Yikes. I looked about five years old!

I hopped off the toilet seat and hurried downstairs.

"Hello, Mikey," Mum said, squeezing me and giving me a big kiss.

"Hi, Mummy," I said. I couldn't believe how babyish my voice sounded.

Dad sat at the kitchen table, drinking coffee. He put down his mug and held out his arms. "Come give Daddy a good morning kiss," he said.

I sighed and forced myself to run into his arms and kiss him on the cheek. I'd forgotten how many stupid things little kids have to put up with.

I ran out of the kitchen on my little five-year-old legs, through the living room, into the den, and back to the kitchen. Something was missing.

No, some*one* was missing.

Tara.

"Sit still for a minute, sweetie," Mum said, scooping me up and plopping me into a chair. "Want some cereal?"

"Where's Tara?" I demanded.

"Who?" Mum replied.

"Tara," I repeated.

Mum glanced at Dad. Dad shrugged.

"You know," I persisted. "My little sister."

Mum smiled. "Oh, *Tara*," she said, seeming to understand at last.

She glanced at Dad and mouthed, "Invisible friend."

"Huh?" Dad said out loud. "He has an invisible friend?"

Mum frowned at him and gave me a bowl of cereal. "What does your friend Tara look like, Mikey?"

I didn't answer her. I was too shocked to speak.

They don't know who I'm talking about! I realized.

Tara don't exist. She hasn't been born yet!

For a brief moment, I felt a thrill. No Tara! I could go through this whole day without ever seeing, hearing, or smelling Tara the Terrible! How totally awesome!

But then the real meaning of this sank in.

One Webster kid had disappeared.

I was next.

After I'd finished my cereal, Mum took me upstairs to get dressed. She put on my shirt and trousers and socks and shoes. She didn't tie the shoes, though.

"Okay, Mikey," she said. "Let's practise tying your shoes. Remember how we did it yesterday?"

87

She took my shoelaces in her fingers and, as she tied them, chanted. "The bunny hops *around* the tree and ducks *under* the bush. Remember?"

She sat back to watch me try to tie my other shoe. I could tell by the look on her face she didn't expect me to get very far.

I bent over and easily tied the shoe. I didn't have time to fool around with this stuff.

Mum stared at me in amazement.

"Come on, Mum, let's get going," I said, straightening up.

"Mikey!" Mum cried. "You did it! You tied your shoe for the first time!" She grabbed me and hugged me hard. "Wait till I tell Daddy!"

I followed her downstairs, rolling my eyes.

So I tied my shoe. Big deal!

"Honey!" Mum called. "Mikey tied his shoe— all by himself!"

"Hey!" Dad cried happily. He held up one hand so I could slap him five. "That's my big boy!"

This time I saw him mouth to Mum: "Took him long enough!"

I was too worried to be insulted.

Mum walked me to nursery school. She told my teacher that I'd learned to tie my shoe. Big excitement all around.

I had to sit around that stupid nursery all morning, finger-painting and singing the ABC song.

I knew I had to get back to that antique store. It was all I could think about.

I've *got* to change that cuckoo clock, I thought desperately. Who knows? Tomorrow I might not know how to walk.

But how would I get there? It had been hard enough to get into town as a second-grader. As a five-year-old, it would be nearly impossible.

And, besides, even if I could get on the bus without anybody asking questions, I didn't have any money with me.

I glanced at the teacher's purse. Maybe I could steal a couple of quarters from her. She'd probably never know.

But if she caught me, I'd be in really big trouble. And I had enough trouble now.

I decided to sneak on to the bus somehow. I knew I could find a way.

When the nursery torture was finally over for the day, I raced out of the building to catch the bus—

—and bumped smack into Mum.

"Hi, Mikey," she said. "Did you have a nice day?"

I forgot that she picked me up every day from nursery school.

She took my hand in her iron grip. There was no escape.

At least I'm here, I thought when I woke up the next morning. At least I'm still alive.

But I'm four years old.

Time is running out.

Mum waltzed into my room, singing, "Good morning to you, good morning to you, good morning dear Mikey, good morning to you! Ready for playgroup?"

Yuck. Playgroup.

Things kept getting worse and worse.

I couldn't take it any more. Mum dropped me off at playgroup with a kiss and her usual, "Have a nice day, Mikey!"

I stalked to the nearest corner and sat. I watched the other little kids play. I refused to do anything. No singing. No painting. No sandbox. No games for me.

"Michael, what's the matter with you today?" the teacher, Ms Sarton asked. "Don't you feel well?"

"I feel okay," I told her.

"Well, then, why aren't you playing?" She studied me for a minute, then added, "I think you need to play."

Without asking my permission or anything, she picked me up, carried me outside, and dumped me in the sandbox.

"Mona will play with you," she said brightly.

Mona was very cute when she was four. Why didn't I remember that?

Mona didn't say anything to me. She concentrated on the sand igloo she was building—at least I *think* it was supposed to be an igloo. It was round, anyway. I started to say hi to her, but suddenly felt shy.

Then I caught myself. Why should I feel bashful with a four-year-old girl?

Anyway, I reasoned, she hasn't seen me in my underwear yet. That won't happen for another eight years.

"Hi, Mona," I said. I cringed when I heard the babyish playgroup voice that came out of my mouth. But everyone else seemed to be used to it.

Mona turned up her nose. "Eeew," she sniffed. "A boy. I hate boys."

"Well," I squeaked in my little boy voice, "if that's the way you feel, forget I said anything."

91

Mona stared at me now, as if she didn't quite understand what I had said.

"You're stupid," she said.

I shrugged and began to draw swirls in the sand with my chubby little finger. Mona dug a moat around her sand igloo. Then she stood up. "Don't let anybody smash my sand castle," she ordered.

So it wasn't an igloo. Guess I was wrong.

"Okay," I agreed.

She toddled away. A few minutes later she returned, carrying a bucket.

She carefully poured a little water into her sand castle moat. She dumped the rest on my head.

"Stupid boy!" she squealed, running away.

I rose and shook my wet head like a dog. I felt a strange urge to burst into tears and run to the teacher for help, but I fought it.

Mona stood a few metres away from me, ready to run. "*Nyah nyah!*" she taunted. "Come and get me, Mikey!"

I pushed my wet hair out of my face and stared at Mona.

"You can't catch me!" she called.

What could I do? I had to chase after her.

I began to run. Mona screamed and raced to a tree by the playground fence. Another girl stood there. Was that Ceecee?

She wore thick glasses with pink rims, and underneath, a pink eyepatch.

I'd forgotten about that eyepatch. She'd had to wear it until halfway through first grade.

Mona screamed again and clutched at Ceecee. Ceecee clutched her back and screamed, too.

I stopped in front of the tree. "Don't worry. I won't hurt you," I assured them.

"Yes you will!" Mona squealed. "Help!"

I sat down on the grass to prove I didn't want to hurt them.

"He's hurting us! He's hurting us!" the girls shouted. They unclutched their hands and jumped on top of me.

"Ow!" I cried.

"Hold his arms!" Mona ordered. Ceecee obeyed. Mona started tickling me under the arms.

"Stop it!" I begged. It was torture. "Stop it!"

"No!" Mona cried. "That's what you get for trying to catch us!"

"I . . . didn't . . ." I had trouble getting the words out while she tickled me. "I didn't . . . try to . . ."

"Yes you did!" Mona insisted.

I'd forgotten that Mona used to be so bossy. It made me think twice. If I ever make it back to my real age, I thought, maybe I won't like Mona so much any more.

"Please stop," I begged again.

"I'll stop," Mona said. "But only if you promise something."

"What?"

"You have to climb that tree." She pointed to the tree by the fence. "Okay?"

I stared at the tree. Climbing it wouldn't be such a big deal. "Okay," I agreed. "Just get off me!"

Mona stood up. Ceecee let go of my arms.

I climbed to my feet and brushed the grass off my trousers.

"You're scared," Mona taunted.

"I am not!" I replied. What a brat! She was almost as bad as Tara!

Now Mona and Ceecee chanted, "Mikey is scared. Mikey is scared."

I ignored them. I grabbed the lowest branch of the tree and hauled myself up. It was harder than I thought it would be. My four-year-old body wasn't very athletic.

"Mikey is scared. Mikey is scared."

"Shut up!" I yelled down at them. "Can't you see that I'm climbing the stupid tree? It doesn't make sense to tease me about being scared."

They both gave me that blank look Mona had given me before. As if they didn't understand what I was saying.

"Mikey is scared," they chanted again.

I sighed and kept climbing. My hands were so small, it was hard to grip the branches. One of my feet slipped.

Then a terrible thought popped into my head.

Wait a minute.

I shouldn't be doing this.

Isn't playgroup the year I broke my arm?

YEEEEOOOOOOWWWWW!

Morning again.

I yawned and opened my eyes. I shook my left arm, the one I broke climbing that stupid tree the day before.

The arm felt fine. Perfectly normal. Completely healed.

I must have gone back in time again, I thought. That's the good part about this messed-up time thing: I didn't have to wait for my arm to heal.

I wondered how far back I'd gone.

The sun poured in through the window of Tara's—or my—room. It cast a weird shadow across my face: a striped shadow.

I tried to roll out of bed. My body slammed against something.

What was that? I rolled back to look.

Bars!

I was surrounded by bars! Was I in jail?

I tried to sit up so I could see better. It wasn't as

easy as usual. My stomach muscles seemed to have grown weak.

At last I managed to sit up and look around.

I wasn't in jail. I was in a cot!

Crumpled up beside me was my old yellow blankie with the embroidered duck on it. I sat beside a small pile of stuffed animals. I was wearing a tiny white undershirt, and—

Oh, no.

I shut my eyes in horror.

It can't be. Please don't let it be true! I prayed.

I opened my eyes and checked to see if my prayer had come true.

It hadn't.

I was wearing a nappy.

A nappy!

How young am I now? How far back in time did I go? I wondered.

"Are you awake, Mikey?"

Mum came into the room. She looked pretty young. I didn't remember ever seeing her this young before.

"Did you get lots of sleep, sweetie pie?" Mum asked. She clearly expected no answer from me. Instead, she shoved a bottle of juice into my mouth.

Yuck! A bottle!

I pulled it out of my mouth and clumsily threw it down.

Mum picked it up. "No, no," she said patiently.

"Bad little Mikey. Drink your bottle now. Come on."

She slid it back into my mouth. I *was* thirsty, so I drank the juice. Drinking from a bottle wasn't that bad, once you got used to it.

Mum left the room. I let the bottle drop.

I had to know how old I was. I had to find out how much time I had left.

I grabbed the bars of the cot and pulled myself to my feet.

Okay, I thought. I can stand.

I took a step. I couldn't control my leg muscles very well. I toddled around the cot.

I can walk, I realized. Unsteadily, but at least I can walk.

I must be about one year old!

I fell just then and banged my head against the side of the cot. Tears welled in my eyes. I started wailing, howling.

Mum ran into the room. "What's the matter, Mikey? What happened?"

She picked me up and started patting me on the back.

I couldn't stop crying. It was really embarrassing.

What am I going to do? I thought desperately. In one night, I went back in time three years!

I'm only one year old now. How old will I be tomorrow?

A little shiver ran down my tiny spine.

I've got to find a way to make time go forward again—today! I told myself.

But what can I do?

I'm not even in playgroup any more.

I'm a baby!

Mum said we were going out. She wanted to dress me. Then she uttered the dreaded words.

"I bet I know what's bothering you, Mikey. You probably need your nappy changed."

"No!" I cried. "No!"

"Oh, yes you do, Mikey. Come on . . ."

I don't like to think about what happened after that. I'd rather block it out of my memory.

I'm sure you understand.

When the worst was over, Mum plopped me down in a playpen—more bars—while she bustled around the house.

I shook a rattle. I batted at a model plane hanging over my head. I watched it spin around.

I pressed buttons on a plastic toy. Different noises came out when I pressed different buttons. A squeak. A honk. A moo.

I was bored out of my mind.

Then Mum picked me up again. She bundled

me into a warm sweater and a dopey little knit cap. Baby blue.

"Want to see Daddy?" she cooed at me. "Want to see Daddy and go shopping?"

"Da-da," I replied.

I'd planned to say, "If you don't take me to Anthony's Antiques, I'll throw myself out of my cot and crack my head open."

But I couldn't talk. It was so frustrating!

Mum carried me out to the car. She strapped me into a baby seat in the back. I tried to say, "Not so tight, Mum!" It came out, "No no no no no!"

"Don't give me a hard time now, Mikey," Mum said sharply. "I know you don't like your car seat, but it's the law." She gave the strap an extra tug.

Then she drove into town.

At least there's a chance, I thought. If we're going to meet Dad, we'll be near the antique store. Maybe, just maybe.

Mum parked the car outside Dad's office building. She unstrapped me from the car seat.

I could move again. But not for long. She pulled a pushchair out of the trunk, unfolded it, and strapped me in.

Being a baby really is like being a prisoner, I thought as she wheeled me across the pavement. I never realized how awful it is!

It was lunchtime. A stream of workers flowed out of the office building. Dad appeared and gave Mum a kiss.

He squatted down to tickle me under the chin. "There's my little boy!" he said.

"Can you say hi to your daddy?" Mum prompted me.

"Hi, Da-da," I gurgled.

"Hi, Mikey," Dad said fondly. But when we stood up, he spoke quietly to Mum, as if I couldn't hear. "Shouldn't he being saying more words by now, honey? Ted Jackson's kid is Mikey's age, and he can say whole sentences. He can say 'lightbulb' and 'kitchen' and 'I want my teddy bear.'"

"Don't start that again," Mum whispered angrily. "Mikey is *not* slow."

I squirmed in my pushchair, fuming. Slow! Who said I was slow?

"I didn't say he was slow, honey," Dad went on. "I only said—"

"Yes you did," Mum insisted. "Yes you did! The other night, when he stuffed those peas up his nose, you said you thought we should have him tested!"

I stuffed peas up my nose? I shuddered.

Sure, stuffing peas up your nose is stupid. But I was only a baby. Wasn't Dad getting carried away?

I thought so.

I wished I could tell them I would turn out all right—at least up to the age of twelve. I mean, I'm no genius, but I get mostly A's and B's.

"Can we discuss this later?" Dad said. "I've only got an hour for lunch. If we're going to find a dining room table, we'd better get moving."

"*You* brought it up," Mum sniffed. She wheeled the pushchair smartly around and began to cross the street. Dad followed us.

I let my eyes rove along the shop windows across the street. An apartment building. A pawnshop. A coffee shop.

Then I found what I was looking for: Anthony's Antiques and Stuff.

My heart leaped. The store still existed! I kept my eyes glued to that sign.

Please take me in there, Mum, I silently prayed. Please please please!

Mum steered me down the street. Past the apartment building. Past the pawnshop. Past the coffee shop.

We stopped in front of Anthony's. Dad stood in front of the window, hands in his pockets, gazing through the glass. Mum and I pulled up beside him.

I couldn't believe it. Finally, after all this time—some good luck!

I stared through the window, searching for it.

The clock.

The window display was set up like an old-fashioned living room. My eyes roamed over the furniture: a wooden bookcase, a fringed table lamp, a Persian rug, an overstuffed armchair, and a clock . . . a table clock. Not the cuckoo clock.

Not the right clock.

My heart sank back to its normal low spot in my chest.

It figures, I thought. Here I am, at the antique shop, at last.

And the clock isn't here.

I felt like crying.

I could have cried, too. Easily.

After all, I was a baby. People expected me to cry.

But I didn't. Even though I looked like a baby, I was a twelve-year-old inside. I still had my pride.

Dad stepped to the door and held it open for Mum and me. Mum pushed me inside. I sat strapped into the pushchair.

The shop was jammed with old furniture. A chubby man in his forties strolled down the aisle towards us.

Behind him, down at the end of the aisle, in a corner at the back of the shop, I saw it. The clock. *The* clock.

A squeal of excitement popped out of me. I began to rock in my pram. I was so close!

"May I help you?" the man asked Mum and Dad.

"We're looking for a dining room table," Mum told him.

I had to get out of that pushchair. I had to get to that clock.

I rocked harder, but it was no good. I was strapped in. "Let me out of this thing!" I shouted.

Mum and Dad turned to look at me. "What's he saying?" Dad asked.

"It sounded like 'La ma la ma'," the shopkeeper suggested.

I rocked harder than ever and screamed.

"He hates his pushchair," Mum explained. She leaned down and unbuckled the straps. "I'll hold him for a few minutes. Then he'll quieten down."

I waited until she held me in her arms. Then I screamed again and wriggled as hard as I could.

Dad's face reddened. "Michael, what is wrong with you?"

"Down! Down!" I yelled.

"All right," Mum muttered, setting me down on the floor. "Now please stop screaming."

I quietened down immediately. I tested my wobbly, chubby little legs. They wouldn't get me far, but they were all I had to work with.

"Keep an eye on him," the shopkeeper warned. "A lot of this stuff is breakable."

Mum grabbed my hand. "Come on, Mikey. Let's go look at some tables."

She tried to lead me to a corner of the shop where several wooden tables stood. I whined and squirmed, hoping to get away. Her grip was too tight.

"Mikey, *shh*," she said.

I let her drag me to the tables. I glanced up at the cuckoo clock. It was almost noon.

At noon, I knew, the cuckoo would pop out. It was my only chance to grab the bird and turn it around.

I tugged on Mum's hand. She tightened her grip.

"What do you think of this one, honey?" Dad asked her, rubbing his hand along a dark wood table.

"I think that wood's too dark for our chairs, Herman," Mum said. Another table caught her eye. As she moved towards it, I tried to slip my hand out of hers. No go.

I toddled after her to the second table. I shot another glance at the clock. The minute hand moved.

Two minutes to twelve.

"We can't be too picky, honey," Dad said. "The Bergers are coming over Saturday night—two days from now—for a dinner party. We can't have a dinner party without a dining room table!"

"I *know* that, dear. But there's no point in buying a table we don't like."

Dad's voice began to rise. Mum's mouth got that hard, set look to it.

Aha. A fight. This was my chance.

Dad was shouting. "Why don't we just spread a blanket out on the floor and make them eat there? We'll call it a picnic!"

Mum finally relaxed her grip on my hand.

I slipped away and toddled as fast as I could towards the clock.

The clock's minute hand moved again.

I toddled faster.

I heard my parents shouting at each other. "I won't buy an ugly table, and that's that!" Mum cried.

Please don't let them notice me, I prayed. Not yet.

I reached the cuckoo clock at last. I stood in front of it and stared up at the clock.

The cuckoo's window was far above me, out of reach.

The minute hand clicked again. The clock's gong sounded.

The cuckoo's window slid open. The cuckoo popped out.

It cuckooed once.

It cuckooed twice.

I stared up at it, helpless.

A twelve-year-old boy trapped in a baby's body.

I stared grimly up at the clock.

Somehow, I had to reach that cuckoo.

Somehow, I *had* to turn it around.

Cuckoo! Cuckoo!

Three, four.

I knew that once it reached twelve, I was doomed.

The cuckoo bird would disappear.

And so would my last chance to save myself.

In a day or so, I would disappear. Disappear for ever.

Frantic, I glanced around for a ladder, a stool, anything.

The closest thing was a chair.

I toddled over to the chair and pushed it towards the clock. It moved a few centimetres.

I leaned, putting all my weight into it. I figured I weighed about twenty pounds.

But it was enough. The chair began to slide across the floor.

Cuckoo! Cuckoo! Five, six.

I shoved the chair up against the clock. The seat of the chair came up to my chin.

I tried to pull myself up on to the seat. My arms were too weak.

I planted a baby shoe against the chair leg. I boosted myself up. I grabbed a spindle at the back of the chair and heaved my body on to the seat.

I made it!

Cuckoo! Cuckoo! Seven, eight.

I got to my knees. I got to my feet.

I reached up to grab the cuckoo. I stretched as tall as I could.

Cuckoo! Cuckoo! Nine, ten.

Reaching, reaching.

Then I heard the shopkeeper shout, "Somebody grab that baby!"

I heard pounding footsteps.

They were running to get me.

I strained to reach the cuckoo. Just another inch . . .

Cuckoo!

Eleven.

Mum grabbed me. She lifted me up.

For one second, the cuckoo flashed within my reach.

I grasped it and turned the head around.

Cuckoo!

Twelve.

The cuckoo slid back into the clock, facing the right way.

Forward.

I wriggled out of Mum's arms, landing on the chair.

"Mikey, what's got into you?" she cried. She tried to grab me again.

I dodged her. I reached around to the side of the clock.

I saw the little dial that told the year. I felt for the button that controlled it. I could just reach it, standing on the chair.

I slammed my hand on the button, carefully watching the years whiz by.

I heard the shopkeeper yelling, "Get that baby away from my clock!"

Mum grabbed me again, but I screamed. I screamed so loudly, it startled her. She let her hands drop.

"Mikey, let go of that!" Dad ordered.

I took my hand off the button. The dial showed the right year. The present year. The year I turned twelve.

Mum made another grab for me. This time I let her pick me up.

It doesn't matter what happens now, I thought. Either the clock will work, and I'll go back to being twelve again . . .

. . . or else it won't work. And then what?

Then I'll disappear. Vanish in time. For ever.

I waited.

"I'm so sorry," Dad said to the shopkeeper. "I hope the baby didn't damage the clock."

The muscles in my neck tensed.

Nothing was happening. Nothing.

I waited another minute.

The shopkeeper inspected the clock. "Everything seems okay," he told Dad. "But he's changed the year. I'll have to change it back."

"NO!" I wailed. "No! Don't!"

"That boy could use a little discipline, if you ask me," the shopkeeper said.

He reached his hand around the side of the clock and started to set back the year.

"Nooo!" I wailed. "Nooo!"

That's it, I realized. I'm doomed. I'm a goner.

But the shopkeeper never touched the button.

A bright white light flashed. I felt dizzy, stunned. I blinked. And blinked again.

Several seconds passed before I could see anything.

I felt cool, damp air. I smelled at a musty odour. A garage smell.

"Michael? Do you like it?" Dad's voice.

I blinked. My eyes adjusted. I saw Dad and Mum. Looking older. Looking *normal.*

We were standing in the garage. Dad was holding a shiny new 21-speed bike.

Mum frowned. "Michael, are you feeling all right?"

They were giving me the bike. It was my birthday!

The clock worked! I'd brought myself back to the present!

Almost to the present. Up to my twelfth birthday.

Close enough.

I felt so happy, I thought I'd explode.

I threw myself at Mum and hugged her hard. Then I hugged Dad.

"Wow," Dad gushed. "I guess you really *do* like the bike!"

I grinned. "I love it!" I exclaimed. "I love everything! I love the whole world!"

Mainly, I loved being twelve again. I could walk! I could talk! I could ride the bus by myself!

Whoa! Wait a minute, I thought. It's my birthday.

Don't tell me I have to live through it *again*.

I tensed my shoulders and steeled myself for the horrible day to come.

It's worth it, I told myself. It's worth it if it means time will go forward again, the way it's supposed to.

I knew too well what would happen next.

Tara.

She'd try to get on my bike. The bike would fall over and get scratched.

Okay, Tara, I thought. I'm ready. Come and do your worst.

I waited.

Tara didn't come.

In fact, she didn't seem to be around at all.

She wasn't in the garage. No sign of her.

Mum and Dad *oohed* and *ahhed* over the bike. They didn't act as if anything was wrong. Or anyone was missing.

"Where's Tara?" I asked them.

They looked up.

"Who?" They stared at me.

"Did you invite her to your party?" Mum asked. "I don't remember sending an invitation to a Tara."

Dad grinned at me. "Tara? Is that some girl you have a crush on, Michael?"

"No," I answered, turning red.

It was as if they'd never heard of Tara. Never heard of their own daughter.

"You'd better go upstairs and get ready for your party, Michael," Mum suggested. "The kids will be here soon."

"Okay." I stumbled into the house, dazed.

"Tara?" I called.

Silence.

Could she be hiding somewhere?

I searched through the house. Then I checked her room. I threw open the door. I expected to see a messy, all-pink girl's room with a white canopy bed.

Instead, I saw two twin beds, neatly made with plaid covers. A chair. An empty closet. No personal stuff.

Not Tara's room.

A guest room.

Wow. I was amazed.

No Tara. Tara doesn't exist.

How did that happen?

I wandered into the den, looking for the cuckoo clock.

It wasn't there.

For a second, I felt a shock of fear. Then I calmed down.

Oh, yeah, I remembered. We don't have the clock yet. Not on my birthday. Dad bought it a couple of days later.

But I still didn't understand. What had happened to my little sister? Where was Tara?

My friends arrived for the party. We played CDs and ate tortilla chips. Ceecee pulled me into a corner and whispered that Mona had a crush on me.

Wow. I glanced at Mona. She turned a little pink and glanced away, shyly.

Tara wasn't there to embarrass me. It made a big difference.

My friends had all brought presents. I actually opened them myself. No Tara to open my presents before I got to them.

At cake time, I carried the cake into the dining room and set it in the middle of the table. No problem. I didn't fall and make a fool out of myself.

Because Tara wasn't there to trip me.

It was the greatest birthday party I'd ever had. It was probably the greatest *day* I'd ever lived— because Tara wasn't there to ruin it.

I could get used to this, I thought.

A few days later, the cuckoo clock was delivered to our house.

"Isn't it great?" Dad gushed, as he had the first time. "Anthony sold me the clock cheap. He said he'd discovered a tiny flaw on it."

The flaw. I'd almost forgotten about it.

We still didn't know what it was. But I couldn't help wondering if it had something to do with Tara's disappearance.

Maybe the clock didn't work perfectly in some way? Maybe it had somehow left Tara behind?

I hardly dared to touch the clock. I didn't want to set off any more weird time trips.

But I had to know what had happened.

I carefully studied the face of the clock again, and all the decorations. Then I stared at the dial that showed the year.

It was properly set at the current year.

Without really thinking about it, I scanned twelve places down the dial to find the year I was born.

There it was.

Then I scanned my eyes back up the dial. 1984. 1985. 1986. 1987. 1989 . . .

Wait a second.

Didn't I just skip a year?

I checked the dates again.

Nineteen-eighty-eight was missing. There was no 1988 on the dial.

And 1988 was the year Tara was born!

"Dad!" I cried. "I found the flaw! Look—there's a year missing on the dial."

Dad patted me on the back. "Good job, son! Wow, isn't that funny?"

To him it was just a funny mistake.

He had no idea his daughter had never been born.

I suppose there's some way to go back in time and get her.

I guess I probably ought to do that.

And I will.

Really.

One of these days.

Maybe.

The Girl Who
Cried Monster

I love scaring my little brother, Randy. I tell him scary stories about monsters until he begs me to stop. And I'm always teasing him by pretending to see monsters everywhere.

I suppose that's why no one believed me the day I saw a *real* monster.

I suppose that's why no one believed me until it was too late, and the monster was right in my own house.

But I'd better not tell the ending of my story at the beginning.

My name is Lucy Dark. I'm twelve. I live with my brother, Randy, who is six, and my parents in a medium-sized house in a medium-sized town called Timberland Falls.

I don't know why it's called Timberland Falls. There are a few forests outside town, but no one cuts the trees down for timber. And there aren't any waterfalls.

So, why Timberland Falls?

It's a mystery.

We have a redbrick house at the end of our street. There's a tall, overgrown hedge that runs along the side of our house and separates our garden from the Killeens' garden next door. Dad's always talking about how he should trim the hedge, but he never does.

We have a small front garden and a pretty big back garden with a lot of tall, old trees in it. There's an old sassafras tree in the middle of the garden. It's cool and shady under the tree. That's where I like sitting with Randy when there's nothing better to do, and see if I can scare the socks off him!

It isn't very hard. Randy gets scared easily.

He looks a lot like me, even though he's a boy. He's got straight black hair just like mine, only I wear mine longer. He's short for his age, like me, and just a little bit chubby.

He has a round face, rounder than mine, and big black eyes, which really stand out since we both have such pale skin.

Mum says Randy has longer eyelashes than mine, which makes me kind of jealous. But my nose is straighter, and my teeth don't stick out as much when I smile. So I suppose I shouldn't complain.

Anyway, on a hot afternoon a couple of weeks ago, Randy and I were sitting under the old sassafras tree, and I was getting ready to scare him to death.

I really didn't have anything better to do. As soon as summer came around this year and school finished, most of my really good friends went away for the summer. I was stuck at home, and so I got pretty lonely.

Randy is usually a total pain. But at least he is somebody to talk to. And someone I can *scare*.

I have a really good imagination. I can dream up the most amazing monsters. And I can make them sound really real.

Mum says with my imagination, maybe I'll be a writer when I grow up.

I really don't know about that.

I *do* know that it doesn't take a whole lot of imagination to frighten Randy.

Usually all I have to do is tell him there's a monster trying on his clothes upstairs in his wardrobe, and Randy turns even whiter than normal and starts shaking all over.

The poor kid. I can even make his teeth chatter. It's unbelievable.

I leaned back against the smooth part of the tree trunk and rested my hands on the grass, and closed my eyes. I was dreaming up a good story to tell my brother.

The grass felt soft and moist against my bare feet. I dug my toes into the earth.

Randy was wearing denim shorts and a plain white sleeveless T-shirt. He was lying on his side, pulling up blades of grass with one hand.

"Did you ever hear about the Timberland Falls toe-biter?" I asked him, brushing a spider off my white tennis shorts.

"Huh?" He kept pulling up blades of grass one by one, making a little pile.

"There was this monster called the Timberland Falls toe-biter," I told Randy.

"Aw, please, Lucy," he whined. "You said you wouldn't make up any more monster stories."

"No, I'm not!" I told him. "This story isn't made up. It's true."

He looked up at me and made a face. "Yeah. Of course."

"No. Really," I insisted, staring hard into his round, black eyes so he'd know I was sincere. "This is a true story. It really happened. Here. In Timberland Falls."

Randy pulled himself up to a sitting position. "I think I'll go inside and read some comics," he said, tossing down a handful of grass.

Randy has a big comic collection. But they're all Disney comics and *Archie* comics because the superhero comics are too scary for him.

"The toe-biter showed up one day right next door," I told Randy. I knew once I started the story, he wouldn't leave.

"At the Killeens'?" he asked, his eyes growing wider.

"Yeah. He arrived in the middle of the afternoon. The toe-biter isn't a night monster, you see. He's a day monster. He strikes when the sun is high in the sky. Just like now."

I pointed up through the shimmering tree leaves to the sun, which was high overhead in a clear summer-blue sky.

"A d-day monster?" Randy asked. He turned his head to look at the Killeens' house rising up on the other side of the hedge.

"Don't be scared. It happened a couple of summers ago," I continued. "Becky and Lilah were over there. They were swimming. You know. In that plastic pool that their mum inflates for them. The one that half the water always spills out of."

"And a monster came?" Randy asked.

"A toe-biter," I told him, keeping my expression very serious and lowering my voice nearly to a whisper. "A toe-biter came crawling across their back garden."

"Where'd he come from?" Randy asked, leaning forward.

I shrugged. "No one knows. You see, the thing about toe-biters is they're very hard to see when they crawl across grass. Because they make themselves the exact colour of the grass."

127

"You mean they're green?" Randy asked, rubbing his pudgy nose.

I shook my head. "They're only green when they creep and crawl over the grass," I replied. "They change their colour to match what they're walking on. So you can't see them."

"Well, how big is it?" Randy asked thoughtfully.

"Big," I said. "Bigger than a dog." I watched an ant crawl up my leg, then flicked it off. "No one really knows how big because this monster blends in so well."

"So what happened?" Randy asked, sounding a bit breathless. "I mean to Becky and Lilah." Again he glanced over at the Killeens' grey-tiled house.

"Well, they were in their little plastic pool," I continued. "You know. Splashing around. And I think Becky was lying on her back and had her feet hanging over the side of the pool. And the monster scampered over the grass, nearly invisible. And it saw Becky's toes dangling in the air."

"And—and Becky didn't see the monster?" Randy asked.

I could see he was starting to get really pale and trembly.

"Toe-biters are just so hard to see," I said, keeping my eyes locked on Randy's, keeping my face very straight and solemn.

I took a deep breath and let it out slowly. Just to build up suspense. Then I continued the story.

"Becky didn't notice anything at first. Then she felt a kind of *tickling* feeling. She thought it was the dog licking at her toes. She kicked a little and told the dog to go away.

"But then it didn't tickle so much. It started to hurt. Becky shouted for the dog to stop. But the hurting got even worse. It felt as if the dog was chewing on her toes, with very sharp teeth.

"It started to hurt a lot. So Becky sat up and pulled her feet into the pool. And . . . when she looked down at her left foot, she saw it."

I stopped and waited for Randy to ask.

"Wh-what?" he asked finally, in a shaky voice. "What did she see?"

I leaned forward and brought my mouth close to his ear. "All the toes were missing from her left foot," I whispered.

"No!" Randy screamed. He jumped to his feet. He was as pale as a ghost, and he looked really scared. "That's not true!"

I shook my head solemnly. I forced myself not to crack a smile. "Ask Becky to take off her left shoe," I told him. "You'll see."

"No! You're lying!" Randy wailed.

"Ask her," I said softly.

And then I glanced down at my feet, and my

129

eyes popped wide with horror. "R-R-Randy—look!" I stammered and pointed with a trembling hand down to my feet.

Randy uttered a deafening scream when he saw what I was pointing at.

All the toes on my left foot were missing.

"*Waaaaiiiii!*"

Randy let out another terrified wail. Then he took off, running full speed to the house, crying for Mum.

I took off after him. I didn't want to get into trouble for scaring him again.

"Randy—wait! Wait! I'm okay!" I shouted, laughing.

Of course I had my toes buried in the earth.

He should've been able to work that out.

But he was too scared to think straight.

"Wait!" I called after him. "I didn't get to show you the monster in the tree!"

He heard that. He stopped and turned round, his face still all twisted with fright. "Huh?"

"There's a monster up in the tree," I said, pointing to the sassafras tree we'd just been sitting under. "A tree monster. I saw it!"

"No way!" he screamed, and started running again to the house.

131

"I'll show it to you!" I called, cupping my hands around my mouth so he'd hear me.

He didn't look back. I watched him stumble up the steps to the back door and disappear into the house. The screen door slammed hard behind him.

I stood staring at the back of the house, waiting for Randy to poke his frightened head out again. But he didn't.

I burst out laughing. I mean, the toe-biter was one of my best creations. And then digging my toes into the earth and pretending the monster had got me, too—*what a riot*!

Poor Randy. He was just too easy a victim.

And now he was probably in the kitchen, squealing on me to Mum. That meant that really soon I'd be in for another lecture about how it wasn't nice to scare my little brother and fill him full of scary monster stories.

But what else was there to do?

I stood there staring at the house, waiting for one of them to call me in. Suddenly a hand grabbed my shoulder hard from behind. "*Gotcha!*" a voice growled.

"Oh!" I cried out and nearly jumped out of my skin.

A monster!

I spun round—and stared at the laughing face of my friend Aaron Messer.

Aaron giggled his high-pitched giggle till he had tears in his eyes.

I shook my head, frowning. "You didn't scare me," I insisted.

"Oh. Sure," he replied, rolling his blue eyes. "That's why you screamed for help!"

"I *didn't* scream for help," I protested. "I just cried out a little. In surprise. That's all."

Aaron chuckled. "You thought it was a monster. Admit it."

"A monster?" I said, sneering. "Why would I think that?"

"Because that's all you think about," he said smugly. "You're obsessed."

"Oooh. Big word!" I teased him.

He made a face at me. Aaron is my only friend who stuck around this summer. His parents are taking him somewhere out west in a few months. But in the meantime he's stuck like me, just hanging around, trying to fill in the time.

Aaron is about a foot taller than me. But who isn't? He has curly red hair and freckles all over his face. He's very skinny, and he wears long, baggy shorts that make him look even skinnier.

"I just saw Randy run into the house. Why was he crying like that?" Aaron asked, glancing at the house.

I could see Randy at the kitchen window, staring out at us.

"I think he saw a monster," I told Aaron.

"Huh? Not monsters again!" Aaron cried. He gave me a playful shove. "Get out of here, Lucy!"

"There's one up in that tree," I said seriously, pointing.

Aaron turned around to look. "You're so stupid," he said, grinning.

"No. Really," I insisted. "There's a really ugly monster. I think it's trapped up there in that tree."

"Lucy, stop it," Aaron said.

"That's what Randy saw," I continued. "That's what made him run screaming into the house."

"You see monsters everywhere," Aaron said. "Don't you ever get tired of it?"

"I'm not kidding this time," I told him. My chin trembled, and my expression turned to outright fear as I gazed over Aaron's shoulder at the broad, leafy sassafras tree. "I'll prove it to you."

"Yeah. Of course," Aaron replied with his usual sarcasm.

"Really. Go and get that broom." I motioned to the broom leaning against the back of the house.

"Huh? What for?" Aaron asked.

"Go and get the broom," I insisted. "We'll see if we can get the monster down from the tree."

134

"Uh . . . why do we want to do *that*?" Aaron asked. He sounded very hesitant. I could see that he was starting to wonder if I was being serious or not.

"So you'll believe me," I said seriously.

"I don't *believe* in monsters," Aaron replied. "You know that, Lucy. Save your monster stories for Randy. He's just a kid."

"Will you believe me if one drops out of that tree?" I asked.

"Nothing is going to drop out of that tree. Except maybe some leaves," Aaron said.

"Go and get the broom and we'll see," I said.

"Okay. Fine." He went trotting towards the house.

I grabbed the broom out of his hand when he brought it over. "Come on," I said, leading the way to the tree. "I hope the monster hasn't climbed away."

Aaron rolled his eyes. "I can't believe I'm going along with this, Lucy. I must be *really* bored!"

"You won't be bored soon," I promised. "If the tree monster is still up there."

We stepped into the shade of the tree. I moved close to the trunk and gazed up into its leafy green branches. "Whoa. Stay right there." I put my hand on Aaron's chest, holding him back. "It could be dangerous."

"Give me a break," he muttered under his breath.

"I'll try to shake the branch and bring it down," I said.

"Let me get this straight," Aaron said. "You expect me to believe that you're going to take the broom, shake a tree branch, and a monster is going to come tumbling down from up there?"

"Uh-huh." I could see that the broom handle wasn't quite long enough to reach. "I'm going to have to climb up a little," I told Aaron. "Just watch out, okay?"

"Ooh, I'm shaking. I'm *sooo* scared!" Aaron cried, making fun of me.

I shinned up the trunk and pulled myself onto the lowest limb. It took me a while because I had the broom in one hand.

"See any scary monsters up there?" Aaron asked smugly.

"It's up there," I called down, fear creeping into my voice. "It's trapped up there. It's . . . very angry, I think."

Aaron sniggered. "You're so stupid."

I pulled myself up to a kneeling position on the limb. Then I raised the broom in front of me.

I lifted it up to the next branch. Higher. Higher.

Then, holding on tightly to the trunk with my free hand, I raised the broom as far as it would go—and pushed it against the tree limb.

Success!

I lowered my eyes immediately to watch Aaron.

He let out a deafening shriek of horror as the monster toppled from the tree and landed right on his chest.

Well, actually it wasn't a monster that landed with a soft, crackly thud on Aaron's chest.

It was a ratty old bird's nest that some blue jays had built two springs ago.

But Aaron wasn't expecting it. So it gave him a really good scare.

"Gotcha!" I proclaimed after climbing down from the tree.

He scowled at me. His face was a little purple, which made his freckles look really weird. "You and your monsters," he muttered.

That's exactly what my mum said about ten minutes later. Aaron had gone home, and I'd come into the kitchen and pulled a carton of juice out of the fridge.

Sure enough, Mum appeared in the doorway, her eyes hard and steely, her expression grim. I could see straight away that she was ready to give her "Don't Scare Randy" lecture.

I leaned back against the counter and pretended to listen. The basic idea of the lecture was that my stories were doing permanent harm to my delicate little brother. That I should be encouraging Randy to be brave instead of making him terrified that monsters lurked in every corner.

"But Mum—I saw a *real* monster under the hedge this morning!" I said.

I don't really know why I said that. I suppose I just wanted to interrupt the lecture.

Mum got really exasperated. She threw up her hands and sighed. She has straight, shiny black hair, like Randy and me, and she has green eyes, cat eyes, and a small, feline nose. Whenever Mum starts in on me with one of her lectures, I always picture her as a cat about to pounce.

Don't get me wrong. She's very pretty. And she's a good mum, too.

"I'm going to discuss this with your dad tonight," she said. "Your dad thinks this monster obsession is just a phase you're going through. But I'm not so sure."

"*Life* is just a phase I'm going through," I said softly.

I thought it was pretty clever. But she just glared at me.

Then she reminded me that if I didn't hurry, I'd be late for my Reading Rangers meeting.

139

I glanced at the clock. She was right. My appointment was for four o'clock.

Reading Rangers is a summer reading course at the town library that Mum and Dad made me enroll in. They said they didn't want me to waste the whole summer. And if I joined this thing at the library, at least I'd read some good books.

The way Reading Rangers works is, I have to go and see Mr Mortman, the librarian, once a week. And I have to give a short report and answer some questions about the book I read that week. I get a gold star for every book I report on.

If I get six gold stars, I get a prize. I think the prize is a book. Big deal, right? But it's just a way to make you read.

I thought I'd read some of the scary mystery novels that all my friends are reading. But no way. Mr Mortman insists on everyone reading "classics". He means *old* books.

"I'm going to skate over," I told my mum, and hurried to my room to get my rollerblades.

"You'd better *fly* over!" my mum called up to me. "Hey," she added a few seconds later, "it looks like rain!"

She was always giving me weather reports.

I passed by Randy's room. He was in there in the dark, no lights, the blinds pulled down. Playing Super Nintendo, as usual.

By the time I got my Rollerblades laced and tied, I had only five minutes to get to the library. Luckily, it was only six or seven blocks away.

I was in big trouble anyway. I had managed to read only four chapters of *Huckleberry Finn*, my book for the week. That meant I was going to have to fake it with Mr Mortman.

I picked the book up from my shelf. It was a new paperback. I wrinkled up some of the pages near the back to make it look as if I'd read that far. I tucked it into my rucksack, along with a pair of trainers. Then I made my way down the stairs—not easy in Rollerblades—and headed for the Timberland Falls town library.

The library was in a ramshackle old house on the edge of the Timberland woods. The house had belonged to some eccentric old hermit. And when he died, he had no family, so he donated the house to the town. They turned it into a library.

Some kids said the house had been haunted. But kids say that about *every* creepy old house. The library *did* look like a perfect haunted house, though.

It was three storeys tall, dark-tiled, with a dark, pointy roof between two stone turrets. The house was set back in the trees, as if hiding there. It was always in the shade, always dark and cold inside.

141

Inside, the old floorboards creaked beneath the thin carpet the town council had put down. The high windows let in very little light. And the old wooden bookcases reached nearly to the ceiling. When I edged my way through the narrow aisles between the tall, dark shelves, I always felt as if they were about to close in on me.

I had this frightening feeling that the shelves would lean in on me, cover me up, and I'd be buried there in the darkness forever. Buried under a thousand pounds of dusty, mildewy old books.

But of course that's silly.

It was just a very old house. Very dark and damp. Very creaky. Not as clean as a library should be. Lots of cobwebs and dust.

Mr Mortman did his best, I suppose. But he was pretty creepy, too.

The thing all us kids hated the most about him was that his hands always seemed to be clammy. He would smile at you with those beady little black eyes of his lighting up on his plump, bald head. He would reach out and shake your hand. And his hand was always *sopping wet*!

When he turned the pages of books, he'd leave clammy fingerprints on the corners. His desktop always had small puddles on the top, moist handprints on the leather desk protector.

He was short and round. With that shiny, bald head and those tiny black eyes, he looked a lot like a mole. A wet-pawed mole.

He spoke in a high, scratchy voice. Nearly always whispered. He wasn't a bad man, really. He seemed to like kids. He wasn't unkind or anything. And he *really* liked books.

He was just weird, that's all. He sat on a tall wooden stool that made him hover over his enormous desk. He kept a deep aluminium pan on the side of his desk. Inside the pan were several little turtles, moving around in a couple of centimetres of water. "My timid friends," I heard him call them once.

Sometimes he'd pick up one of them and hold it in his pudgy fingers, high in the air, until it tucked itself into its shell. Then he'd gently put it down, a pleased smile on his pale, flabby face.

He certainly loved his turtles. I suppose they were okay as pets. But they were pretty smelly. I always tried to sit on the other side of the desk, as far away from the turtle pan as I could get.

Well, I skated to the library as fast as I could. I was only a few minutes late when I skated into the cool shade of the library drive. The sky was clouding over. I sat down on the stone steps and pulled off the rollerblades. Then I quickly slid into my trainers and, carrying my rollerblades, I walked through the front door.

Making my way through the stacks—the tall, narrow shelves at the back of the main reading room—I dropped the skates against the wall. Then I walked quickly through the aisles to Mr Mortman's desk against the back wall.

He heard my footsteps and immediately glanced up from the pile of books he was stamping with a big rubber stamp. The ceiling light made his bald head shine like a lamp. He smiled. "Hi, Lucy," he said in his squeaky voice. "Be right with you."

I said hi and sat down on the folding chair in front of his desk. I watched him stamp the books. He was wearing a grey poloneck sweater, which made him look a lot like his pet turtles.

Finally, after glancing at the big, loudly ticking clock on the wall, he turned to me.

"And what did you read for Reading Rangers this week, Lucy?" He leaned over the desk towards me. I could see wet fingerprints on the dark desktop.

"Uh . . . *Huckleberry Finn*." I pulled the book from my rucksack and dropped it into my lap.

"Yes, yes. A wonderful book," Mr Mortman said, glancing at the paperback in my lap. "Don't you agree?"

"Yes," I said quickly. "I really enjoyed it. I . . . couldn't put it down."

144

That was sort of true. I'd never picked it up—so how could I put it down?

"What did you like best about *Huckleberry Finn*?" Mr Mortman asked, smiling at me expectantly.

"Uh . . . the description," I told him.

I had my Reading Rangers gold star in my T-shirt pocket. And I had a new book in my rucksack—*Frankenstein*, by Mary Shelley.

Maybe I'll read *Frankenstein* out loud to Randy, I thought evilly.

That would probably make his teeth chatter forever!

The late afternoon sun was hidden behind spreading rain clouds. I had walked nearly all the way home when I realized I had forgotten my rollerblades.

So I turned round and went back. I wasn't sure how late the library stayed open. Mr Mortman had seemed to be entirely alone in there. I hoped he hadn't decided to shut up shop early. I really didn't want to leave my new rollerblades in there overnight.

I stopped and stared up at the old library. Deep in the shade, it seemed to stare back at me, its dark windows like black, unblinking eyes.

I climbed the stone steps, then hesitated with my hand on the door. I felt a sudden chill.

Was it just from stepping into the deep shade?

No. It was something else.

I had a funny feeling. A bad feeling.

I get those sometimes. A signal. A moment of unease.

As if something bad is about to happen.

Shaking it off, I pushed open the creaking old door and stepped into the musty darkness of the library.

Shadows danced across the wall as I made my way to the main room. A tree branch tapped noisily against the dust-covered pane of a high window.

The library was silent except for the creaking floorboards beneath my trainers. As I entered the main room, I could hear the steady *tick-tick-tick* of the wall clock.

The lights had all been turned off.

I thought I felt something scamper across my shoe.

A mouse?

I stopped short and glanced down.

Just a dustball clinging to the base of a bookshelf.

Whoa, Lucy, I scolded myself. It's just a dusty old library. Nothing to get spooked about. Don't let your wild imagination take off and lead you into trouble.

Trouble?

I still had that strange feeling. A gentle but insistent gnawing at my stomach. A tug at my chest.

Something isn't right. Something bad is about to happen.

People call them *premonitions*. It's a good word for what I was feeling right then.

I found my rollerblades where I had left them, against the wall at the back of the stacks. I grabbed them, eager to get out of that dark, creepy place.

I headed quickly back towards the entrance, tiptoeing for some reason. But a sound made me stop.

I held my breath. And listened.

It was just a cough.

Peering down the narrow aisle, I could see Mr Mortman hovering over his desk. Well, actually, I could just see part of him—one arm, and some of his face when he leaned to the left.

I was still holding my breath.

The clock *tick-tick-ticked* noisily from across the room. Behind his desk, Mr Mortman's face moved in and out of blue-purple shadows.

The rollerblades suddenly felt heavy. I lowered them silently to the floor. Then my curiosity got the better of me, and I took a few steps towards the front.

Mr Mortman began humming to himself. I didn't recognize the song.

The shadows grew deeper as I approached. Peering down the dark aisle, I saw him holding a large glass jar between his pudgy hands. I was close enough to see that he had a pleasant smile on his face.

Keeping in the shadows, I moved closer.

I like spying on people. It's kind of thrilling, even when they don't do anything very interesting.

Just knowing that you're watching them and they don't know they're being watched is exciting.

Humming to himself, Mr Mortman held the jar in front of his chest and started to unscrew the top. "Some juicy flies, my timid friends," he announced in his high-pitched voice.

So. The jar was filled with flies.

Suddenly, the room grew much darker as clouds rolled over the late afternoon sun. The light from the window dimmed. Grey shadows rolled over Mr Mortman and his enormous desk, as if blanketing him in darkness.

From my hidden perch among the shelves, I watched him prepare to feed his turtles.

But wait.

Something was wrong.

My premonition was coming true.

Something *weird* was happening!

As he struggled to unscrew the jar lid, Mr Mortman's face began to change. His head floated up from his poloneck and started to expand, like a balloon being inflated.

I uttered a silent gasp as I saw his tiny eyes poke out of his head. The eyes bulged bigger and bigger, until they were as big as doorknobs.

The light from the window grew even dimmer.

The entire room was cast in heavy shadows. The shadows swung and shifted.

I couldn't see well at all. It was as if I was watching everything through a dark fog.

Mr Mortman continued to hum, even as his head bobbed and throbbed above his shoulders and his eyes bulged out as if on stems, poking straight up like insect antennae.

And then his mouth began to twist and grow. It opened wide, like a gaping black hole on the enormous, bobbing head.

Mr Mortman sang louder now. An eerie, frightening sound, more like an animal howling than singing.

He pulled the lid off the jar and let it fall to the desk. It clanged loudly as it hit the desktop.

I leaned forward, struggling to see. Squinting hard, I saw Mr Mortman dip his fat hand into the jar. I could hear loud buzzing from the jar. He pulled out a handful of flies.

I could see his eyes bulge even wider.

I could see the gaping black hole that was his mouth.

He held his hand briefly over the turtle cage. I

could see the flies, black dots all over his hand. In his palm. On his short, stubby fingers.

I thought he was going to lower his hand to the aluminium pan. I thought he was going to feed the turtles.

But, instead, he jammed the flies into his own mouth.

I shut my eyes and held my hand over my mouth to keep from throwing up.

Or screaming.

I held my breath, but my heart kept racing.

The shadows lurched and jumped. The darkness seemed to float around me.

I opened my eyes. He was eating another handful of flies, shoving them into his gaping mouth with his fingers, swallowing them whole.

I wanted to shout. I wanted to run.

Mr Mortman, I realized, was a monster.

The shadows seemed to pull away. The sky outside the window brightened, and a grey triangle of light fell over Mr Mortman's desk.

Opening my eyes, I realized I'd been holding my breath. My chest felt as if it were about to burst. I let the air out slowly and took another deep breath.

Then, without glancing again at the front of the room, I turned and ran. My trainers thudded over the creaky floors, but I didn't care.

I had to get out of there as fast as I could.

I bolted out of the front door of the library onto the stone steps, then down the gravel drive. I ran as fast as I could, my arms flying wildly at my sides, my black hair blowing behind me.

I didn't stop until I was a block away.

Then I dropped to the kerb and waited for my heart to stop pounding like a bass drum.

Heavy rain clouds rolled over the sun again. The sky became an eerie yellow-black. An estate car rolled past. Some kids in the back of it called to me, but I didn't raise my head.

I kept seeing the shadowy scene in the library again and again.

Mr Mortman is a monster.

The words echoed nonstop in my mind.

It can't be, I thought, gazing up at the black clouds so low overhead.

I was seeing things. That had to be it.

All the shadows in the dark library. All the swirling darkness.

It was an optical illusion.

It was my wild imagination.

It was a daydream, a silly fantasy.

No! a loud voice in my head cried.

No, Lucy, you *saw* Mr Mortman's head bulge. You *saw* his eyes pop out and grow like hideous toadstools on his ballooning face.

You saw him reach into the fly jar. You heard him humming so happily, so . . . hungrily.

You saw him jam the flies into his mouth. Not one handful, but two.

And maybe he's still in there, eating his fill.

It was dark, Lucy. There were shadows. But you saw what you saw. You saw it all.

Mr Mortman is a monster.

I climbed to my feet. I felt a cold drop of rain on top of my head.

"Mr Mortman is a monster." I said it out loud.

I knew I had to tell Mum and Dad as fast as I

could. "The librarian is a monster." That's what I'd tell them.

Of course, they'll be shocked. Who *wouldn't* be?

Feeling another raindrop on my head, then one on my shoulder, I started jogging for home. I had gone about half a block when I stopped.

The stupid rollerblades! I had left them in the library again.

I turned back. A gust of wind blew my hair over my face. I pushed it back with both hands. I was thinking hard, trying to work out what to do.

Rain pattered softly on the pavement. The cold raindrops felt good on my hot forehead.

I decided to go back to the library and get my skates. This time, I'd make a lot of noise. Make sure Mr Mortman knew someone was there.

If he heard me coming, I decided, he'd act normally. He wouldn't eat flies in front of me. He wouldn't let his eyes bulge and his head grow like that.

Would he?

I stopped as the library came back into view. I hesitated, staring through the drizzling rain at the old building.

Maybe I should wait and come back tomorrow with my dad.

Wouldn't that be a better plan?

No. I decided I wanted my skates. And I was going to get them.

I've always been pretty brave.

The time a bat flew into our house, *I* was the one who yelled and screamed at it and chased it out with a butterfly net.

I'm not afraid of bats. Or snakes. Or bugs.

"Or monsters," I said out loud.

As I walked up to the front of the library, rain pattering softly all around me, I kept telling myself to make a lot of noise. Make sure Mr Mortman knows you're there, Lucy. Call out to him. Tell him you came back because you left your skates.

He won't let you see that he's a monster if he knows you're there.

He won't hurt you or anything if you give him some warning.

I kept reassuring myself all the way up to the dark, old building. I climbed the stone steps hesitantly.

Then, taking a deep breath, I grabbed the doorknob and started to go in.

I turned the knob and pushed, but the door refused to open. I tried again. It took me a while to realize that it was locked.

The library was closed.

The rain pattered softly on the grass as I walked around to the front window. It was high off the ground. I had to pull myself up on the window ledge to look inside.

Darkness. Total darkness.

I felt relieved and disappointed at the same time.

I wanted my skates, but I didn't really want to go back in there. "I'll get them tomorrow," I said out loud.

I lowered myself to the ground. The rain was starting to come down harder, and the wind was picking up, blowing the rain in sheets.

I started to run, my trainers squelching over the wet grass. I ran all the way home. I was totally drenched by the time I came through the front door. My hair was matted down on my head. My T-shirt was soaked through.

"Mum! Dad? Are you home?" I cried.

I ran through the hallway, nearly slipping on the smooth floor, and burst into the kitchen. "A monster!" I cried.

"Huh?" Randy was seated at the kitchen table, snapping a big pile of string beans for Mum. He was the only one who looked up.

Mum and Dad were standing at the kitchen units, rolling little meatballs in their hands. They didn't even turn round.

"A monster!" I screamed again.

"Where?" Randy cried.

"Did you get caught in the rain?" Mum asked.

"Don't you say hi?" Dad asked. "Do you just explode into a room yelling? Don't I get a 'Hi, Dad,' or anything?"

"Hi, Dad," I cried breathlessly. "There's a monster in the library!"

"Lucy, please—" Mum started impatiently.

"What kind of monster?" Randy asked. He had stopped snapping the ends off the beans and was staring hard at me.

Mum finally turned round. "You're soaked!" she cried. "You're dripping all over the floor. Get upstairs and change into some dry clothes."

Dad turned, too, a frown on his face. "Your mother has just washed the floor," he muttered.

157

"*I'm trying to tell you something!*" I shouted, raising my fists in the air.

"No need to scream," Mum scolded. "Get changed. Then tell us."

"But Mr Mortman is a *monster!*" I cried.

"Can't you save the monster stuff till later? I've just got home, and I've got an awful headache," Dad complained. His eyes stared down at the kitchen floor. Small puddles were forming around me on the white linoleum.

"I'm serious!" I insisted. "Mr Mortman—he's really a monster!"

Randy laughed. "He's funny-looking."

"Randy, it's not nice to make fun of people's looks," Mum said crossly. She turned back to me. "See what you're teaching your little brother? Can't you set a good example?"

"But, Mum!"

"Lucy, please get into some dry clothes," Dad pleaded. "Then come down and lay the table, okay?"

I was so frustrated! I tilted my head back and let out an angry growl. "Doesn't anyone here *believe* me?" I cried.

"This really isn't the time for your monster stories," Mum said, turning back to her meatballs. "Larry, you're making them too big," she scolded my father. "They're supposed to be small and delicate."

"But I like *big* meatballs," Dad insisted.

No one was paying any attention to me. I turned and stomped angrily out of the kitchen.

"Is Mr Mortman *really* a monster?" Randy called after me.

"I don't know, and I don't care—about *anything*!" I screamed back. I was just so angry and upset.

They didn't have to ignore me like that.

All they cared about was their stupid meatballs.

Up in my room, I pulled off my wet clothes and tossed them to the floor. I changed into jeans and a tank top.

Is Mr Mortman really a monster?

Randy's question echoed in my head.

Did I imagine the whole thing? Do I just have monsters on the brain?

It had been so dark and shadowy in the library with all the lights turned off. Maybe Mr Mortman didn't eat the flies. Maybe he pulled them out of the jar and fed them to his pet turtles.

Maybe I just imagined that he ate them.

Maybe his head didn't swell up like a balloon. Maybe his eyes didn't pop out. Maybe that was just a trick of the darkness, the dancing shadows, the dim grey light.

Maybe I need glasses.

Maybe I'm crazy and weird.

"Lucy—hurry down and set the table," my dad called up the stairs.

"Okay. Coming." As I made my way downstairs, I felt all mixed up.

I didn't mention Mr Mortman at dinner. Actually, Mum brought him up. "What book did you choose to read this week?" she asked.

"*Frankenstein*," I told her.

Dad groaned. "More monsters!" he cried, shaking his head. "Don't you ever get *enough* monsters? You *see* them wherever you go! Do you have to *read* about monsters, too?"

Dad has a big booming voice. Everything about my dad is big. He looks very tough, with a broad chest and powerful-looking arms. When he shouts, the whole house shakes.

"Randy, you did a great job with the string beans," Mum said, quickly changing the subject.

After dinner, I helped Dad with the dishes. Then I went upstairs to my room to start reading *Frankenstein*. I'd seen the old film of *Frankenstein* on TV, so I knew what it was about. It was about a scientist who builds a monster, and the monster comes to life.

It sounded like my kind of story.

I wondered if it was true.

To my surprise, I found Randy in my room, sitting on my bed, waiting for me. "What do you want?" I asked. I really don't like him messing around in my room.

"Tell me about Mr Mortman," he said. I could

160

tell by his face that he was scared and excited at the same time.

I sat down on the edge of the bed. I realized I was eager to tell someone about what had happened in the library. So I told Randy the whole story, starting with how I had to go back there because I'd left my rollerblades behind.

Randy was squeezing my pillow against his chest and breathing really hard. The story got him pretty scared, I suppose.

I was just finishing the part where Mr Mortman stuffed a handful of flies into his mouth. Randy gasped. He looked ill.

"Lucy!" My dad burst angrily into the room. "What is your *problem*?"

"Nothing, Dad, I—"

"How many times do we have to tell you not to frighten Randy with your silly monster stories?"

"Silly?" I shrieked. "But, Dad—this one is *true!*"

He made a disgusted face and stood there glaring at me. I expected fire to come shooting out of his nostrils at any minute.

"I—I'm not scared. Really!" Randy protested, coming to my defence. But my poor brother was as white as the pillow he was holding, and trembling all over.

"This is your last warning," Dad said. "I mean it, Lucy. I'm *really* angry." He disappeared back downstairs.

I stared at the doorway where he'd been standing.

I'm really angry, too, I thought.

I'm really angry that no one in this family believes me when I'm being serious.

I knew at that moment that I had no choice.

I had to prove that I wasn't a liar. I had to prove that I wasn't making it all up.

I had to *prove* to Mum and Dad that Mr Mortman was a monster.

"What's that?" I asked Aaron.

It was a week later. I had to pass his house to get to the library for my Reading Rangers meeting. I stopped when I saw Aaron in the front garden. He was tossing a blue disc, then catching it when it snapped back at him.

"It's like a Frisbee on a long rubber band," he said. He tossed the disc and it snapped back fast. He missed it and it flew behind him, then snapped back again—and hit him on the back of the head.

"That's not how it's supposed to work exactly," he said, blushing. He started to untangle a knot in the thick rubber band.

"Can I play with you?" I asked.

He shook his head. "No. It's for one person, see?"

"It's a one-person Frisbee?" I asked.

"Yeah. Haven't you seen the adverts on TV?

You play it by yourself. You throw it and then you catch it."

"But what if someone wants to play *with* you?" I demanded.

"You can't," Aaron answered. "It doesn't work that way."

I thought it was pretty stupid. But Aaron seemed to be having a good time. So I said goodbye and continued on to the library.

It was a beautiful, sunny day. Everything seemed bright and cheerful, golden and summer green.

The library, as usual, was bathed in blue shadows. I'd only been back once since that day. Once *very* quickly, to get my rollerblades. I stopped at the kerb, staring up at it. I felt a sudden chill.

The whole world seemed to grow darker here. Darker and colder.

Just my imagination?

We'll see, I thought. We'll see today what's real and what isn't.

I pulled my rucksack off my shoulders and, swinging it by the straps, made my way to the front door. Taking a deep breath, I pushed open the door and stepped inside.

Perched over his desk in the main reading room, Mr Mortman was just finishing with another Reading Rangers member. It was a girl I knew from school, Ellen Borders.

I watched from the end of a long row of books. Mr Mortman was saying goodbye. He handed her a gold star. Then he shook Ellen's hand, and I could see her try not to make a disgusted face. His hand was probably sopping wet, as usual.

She said something, and they both laughed. Very jolly.

Ellen said goodbye and headed towards the doorway. I stepped out to greet her. "What book did you get?" I asked after we had said our hellos.

She held it up for me. "It's called *White Fang*," she said.

"It's about a monster?" I guessed.

She laughed. "No, Lucy. It's about a dog."

I thought I saw Mr Mortman's head lift up when I said the word *monster*.

But I might've imagined that.

I chatted a short while longer with Ellen, who was three books ahead of me this summer. She had only one more to read to get her prize. What a show-off.

I heard the front door close behind her as I took my seat next to Mr Mortman's desk and pulled *Frankenstein* from my bookbag.

"Did you enjoy it?" Mr Mortman asked. He had been studying his turtles, but he turned to face me, a friendly smile on his face.

He was wearing another poloneck, a bright yellow one this time. I noticed that he wore a big, purple ring on one of his pudgy pink fingers. He twirled the ring as he smiled at me.

"It was quite hard," I said. "But I liked it."

I had read more than half of this one. I would have finished it if it didn't have such tiny type.

"Did you enjoy the description in this book, too?" Mr Mortman asked, leaning closer to me over the desk.

My eye caught the big jar of flies on the shelf behind him. It was very full.

"Well, yeah," I said. "I sort of expected more action though."

"What was your favourite part of the book?" Mr Mortman asked.

"The monster!" I answered instantly.

I watched his face to see if he reacted to that word. But he didn't even blink. His tiny black eyes remained locked on mine.

"The monster was really great," I said. I decided to test him. "Wouldn't it be cool if there were *real* monsters, Mr Mortman?"

Again he didn't blink. "Most people wouldn't be very happy about that," he said quietly, twirling his purple ring. "Most people like to get their scares in books or in films. They don't want their scares to be in real life." He chuckled.

I forced myself to chuckle, too.

I took a deep breath and continued my little test. I was trying to catch him out, to reveal that

166

he wasn't really human. "Do you believe that real monsters exist?" I asked.

Not very subtle. I admit it.

But he didn't seem to notice.

"Do I believe that a scientist such as Dr Frankenstein could build a living monster?" Mr Mortman asked. He shook his round, bald head. "We can build robots, but not living creatures."

That wasn't what I meant.

Some other people came into the library. A little girl with her white-haired grandmother. The little girl went skipping to the children's book section. The grandmother picked up a newspaper and carried it to an armchair across the room.

I was very unhappy to see them. I knew that the librarian wouldn't change into a monster while they were here. I was sure he only ate flies when the library was empty. I was going to have to hide somewhere and wait for them to leave.

Mr Mortman reached into his desk drawer, pulled out a gold star, and handed it to me. I thought he was going to shake my hand, but he didn't. "Have you read *Anne of Green Gables*?" he asked, picking up a book from the pile on his desk.

"No," I said. "Does it have monsters in it?"

He threw back his head and laughed, his chins quivering.

I thought I caught a flash of recognition in his eyes. A question. A tiny moment of hesitation.

I thought my question brought something strange to his eyes.

But, of course, again it could have been my imagination.

"I don't think you'll find any monsters in this one," he said, still chuckling. He stamped it with his rubber stamp and handed it to me. The cover was moist from where his fingers had been.

I made an appointment for the same time next week. Then I walked out of the main reading room and pretended to leave the library.

I pulled open the front door and let it slam, but I didn't go out. Instead, I crept back, keeping in the shadows. I stopped at the back wall, hidden by a long row of bookshelves.

Where to hide?

I had to find a safe hiding place. Safe from Mr Mortman's beady eyes. And safe from anyone else who might enter the library.

What was my plan?

Well, I'd been thinking about it all week. But I really didn't have much of a plan. I just wanted to catch him in the act, that's all.

I wanted to see clearly. I wanted to erase all doubts from my mind.

My plan was to hide until the library was empty, to spy on Mr Mortman, to watch him change into a monster and eat flies again.

Then I'd know I wasn't crazy. Then I'd know my eyes hadn't been playing tricks on me.

On the other side of the room, I could hear the little girl's grandmother calling to Mr Mortman. "Do you have any spelling books? Samantha only likes picture books. But I want her to learn to spell."

"Grandma, whisper!" Samantha called harshly. "This is a library, remember! Whisper!"

My eyes searched the long, dark shelves for a hiding place. And there it was. A low bookshelf along the floor near the back was empty. It formed a narrow cave that I could crawl into.

Trying to be as quiet as I could, I got down on my knees, sat down on the shelf, turned, slid my body back, and tucked myself in.

It wasn't really large enough to stretch out. I had to keep my legs folded. My head was pressed hard against the upright board. Not very comfortable. I knew I couldn't stay like this forever.

But it was late afternoon. Maybe Samantha and her grandmother would leave soon. Maybe I wouldn't have to stay tucked on the shelf like a mouldy old book for very long.

My heart was pounding. I could hear Mr Mortman talking softly to Samantha. I could hear the rustle of the old lady's newspaper. I could hear the *tick-tick-tick* of the big wall clock on the front wall.

I could hear every sound, every creak and groan.

I suddenly had to sneeze. My nose tickled like crazy! There was so much dust down here.

I reached up and squeezed my nose hard between my thumb and forefinger. Somehow I managed to stop the sneeze.

My heart was pounding even harder. I could hear it over the *tick-tick-tick* of the clock.

Please leave, I thought, wishing Samantha and her grandmother *out* of there.

Please leave. Please leave. Please leave.

I don't know how long I can stay tucked on this dusty shelf.

My neck was already starting to hurt from being pressed against the shelf. And I felt another sneeze coming on.

"This book is too hard. I need an easier one," Samantha was saying to Mr Mortman.

I heard Mr Mortman mutter something. I heard shuffling feet. Footsteps.

Were they coming this way?

Were they going to see me?

No. They turned and headed back to the children's section on the side.

"I've already read this one," I heard Samantha complain.

Please leave. Please leave. Please leave.

It must have been only a few minutes later

170

when Samantha and her grandmother left, but it seemed like hours to me.

My neck was stiff. My back ached. My legs were tingling, both asleep.

I heard the front door close behind them.

The library was empty now. Except for Mr Mortman and me.

I waited. And listened.

I heard the scrape of his tall stool against the floor. Then I heard his footsteps. He coughed.

It suddenly grew darker. He was turning off the lights.

It's show time! I thought.

He's closing up. Now's the time. Now's the time he'll turn into a monster before my eyes.

I rolled silently off the shelf, onto the floor. Then I pulled myself up to a standing position. Holding onto a higher shelf, I raised one leg, then the other, trying to get the circulation back.

As the overhead lights went out, most of the library was blanketed in darkness. The only light came from the late afternoon sunlight flooding through the window at the front of the room.

Where was Mr Mortman?

I heard him cough again. Then he began to hum to himself.

He was closing up.

Holding my breath, I tiptoed closer to his desk.

I leaned my side against the shelves as I moved, keeping in the shadows.

Whoa.

I suddenly realized Mr Mortman wasn't at his desk.

I heard his footsteps behind me, at the back of the main reading room. Then I heard his shoes thud across the floor of the front entrance.

I froze in place, listening hard, still holding my breath.

Was he leaving?

No.

I heard a loud *click*.

The sound of a lock being turned.

He had locked the front door!

I hadn't planned on that. No way. That was definitely *not* part of my plan.

Frozen in the dark aisle, I realized that I was *locked in* with him!

Now what?

Maybe my plan wasn't exactly the best plan in the world.

Maybe the whole idea was stupid.

You can bet I had plenty of doubts racing through my mind as I heard Mr Mortman return to the main reading room.

My plan, of course, was to prove to myself that I was right, that he was a monster. And then—to run out of the library!

The plan wasn't to be locked in that dark, creepy building with him, unable to escape.

But here I was.

So far, I was okay. He had no idea that anyone else was here with him. No idea that he was being spied on.

Pressed against the tall shelves, I crept along the narrow aisle until I was as close as I dared to go. I could see his entire desk, caught in a deep orange rectangle of light from the high window.

Mr Mortman stepped behind his desk, humming softly to himself. He straightened a pile of books, then shoved it to a corner of the desk.

He pulled open his desk drawer and shuffled things around, searching for something in there.

I crept a little closer. I could see very clearly now. The afternoon sunlight made everything orangey-red.

Mr Mortman tugged at the neck of his poloneck. He rolled some pencils off the desktop into the open desk drawer. Then he shut the drawer.

This is boring, I thought.

This is boring. And normal.

I must have been wrong last week. I must have imagined the whole thing.

Mr Mortman is just a funny little man. He isn't a monster at all.

I sank against the tall shelf, disappointed.

I'd wasted all this time, hiding on that filthy shelf—for nothing.

And now here I was locked in the library after closing time, watching the librarian clear up his desk.

What a thrill!

I've got to get out of here, I thought. I've been really stupid.

But then I saw Mr Mortman reach for the fly jar on the shelf behind him.

I swallowed hard. My heart gave a sudden lurch.

174

A smile crossed Mr Mortman's pudgy face as he put the big glass jar down in front of him. Then he reached across the desk and, with both hands, pulled the rectangular turtle pan closer.

"Dinnertime, my timid friends," he said in his high, scratchy voice. He grinned down at the turtles. He reached into the pan and splashed the water a bit. "Dinnertime, friends," he repeated.

And, then, as I stared without blinking, stared with my jaw dropping lower and lower in disbelief, his face began to change again.

His round head began to swell up.

His black eyes bulged.

His mouth grew until it became an open black pit.

The enormous head bobbed above the yellow poloneck. The eyes swam in front of the head. The mouth twisted, opening and closing like an enormous fish mouth.

I was right! I realized.

Mr Mortman is a monster!

I knew I was right! But no one would believe me.

They'll have to believe me now, I told myself. I'm seeing this so clearly. It's all so bright in the red-orange light.

I'm seeing it. I'm not imagining it.

They'll have to believe me now.

And as I gaped openmouthed at the gross creature the librarian had become, he reached into the fly jar, removed a handful of flies, and shovelled them hungrily into his mouth.

"Dinnertime," he rasped, talking as he chewed.

I could hear the buzz of the flies inside the jar.

They were *alive*! The flies were alive, and he was gobbling them up as if they were chocolates.

I raised my hands and pressed them against the sides of my face as I stared.

"Dinnertime!"

Another handful of flies.

Some of them had escaped. They buzzed loudly around his swollen, bobbing head.

As he chewed and swallowed, Mr Mortman grabbed at the flies in the air, his tiny hands surprisingly quick. He pulled flies out of the air—one, another, another—and popped them into his enormous gorge of a mouth.

Mr Mortman's eyes swam out in front of his face.

For a short, terrifying moment, the eyes stopped. They were staring right at me!

I realized I had leaned too far into the aisle.

Had he spotted me?

I jumped back with a gasp of panic.

The bulging black eyes, like undulating toad-stools, remained in place for another second or two. Then they continued rolling and swimming about.

After a third handful of flies, Mr Mortman closed the jar, licking his lips with a snake-like, pencil-thin tongue.

The buzzing stopped.

The room was silent again except for the ticking clock and my thundering heartbeats.

Now what? I thought.

Is that it?

No.

"Dinnertime, my timid friends," the librarian said in a thin, trembling voice, the voice seeming to bob along with the enormous head.

He reached a hand into the pan and picked up one of the little green-shelled turtles. I could see the turtle's legs racing.

Is he going to feed some flies to the turtles now? I wondered.

Mr Mortman held the turtle higher, studying it with his bulging, rolling eyes. He held it up to the sunlight. The turtle's legs continued to move.

Then he popped the turtle into his mouth.

I heard the crack of the shell as Mr Mortman bit down.

He chewed noisily, several times, making a loud *crunch* with each chew. Then I saw him swallow once, twice, till he got it down.

I'd seen enough.

More than enough.

I turned away. I began to make my way blindly back through the dark aisle. I jogged quickly. I didn't really care if he heard me or not.

I just had to get out of there.

Out into the sunlight and fresh air.

Away from the crunching sound that kept echoing in my ears. The crunch of the turtle shell as Mr Mortman chewed it and chewed it.

Chewed it alive.

I ran from the main reading room, my heart thudding, my legs feeling heavy as stone.

I was gasping for breath when I reached the front entrance. I ran to the door and grabbed the handle.

And then remembered.

The door was locked.

I couldn't get out.

I was locked in.

And, then, as I stood staring straight ahead at the closed door, my hand gripping the brass knob, I heard footsteps. Behind me. Rapid footsteps.

Mr Mortman had heard me.

I was trapped.

I froze in panic, staring at the door until it became a dark blur in front of me.

Mr Mortman's footsteps grew louder behind me.

Help! I uttered a silent plea. *Somebody—help me!*

The librarian would burst into the front entrance any second. And there I'd be. Trapped at the door.

Trapped like a rat. Or like a turtle!

And then what?

Would he grab me up like one of his pets?

Would he crunch me between his teeth?

There had to be a way out of there. There *had* to be!

And, then, staring at the blur of the door, it suddenly came clear to me. It all came back in focus. And I realized that maybe—just maybe—I wasn't trapped at all.

Mr Mortman had locked the door from the inside.

The *inside*.

That meant that maybe I could unlock it and open the door.

If the door locked with a key, then I was stuck.

But if it was just an ordinary lock that you turned . . .

"Hey, is someone out there?" Mr Mortman's raspy voice burst into my thoughts.

My eyes frantically searched the door. I found the lock under the brass knob.

I reached for it.

Please turn. Please turn. Please turn.

The lock turned in my hand with a soft click. The prettiest sound I ever heard!

In a second, I had pulled open the door. In another second, I was out on the stone steps. Then, I was running as fast as I could, running across the front lawn, cutting through some shrubs, diving through a hedge—running for my life!

Gasping for air, I turned halfway down the road. I could see Mr Mortman, a shadowy figure in the library door. He was standing in the doorway, staring out, not moving. Just standing there.

Had he seen me?

Did he know it was me spying on him?

I didn't want to know. I just wanted to get away.

The late afternoon sun was ducking behind the trees, making the shadows long and dark. I lowered my head and ran into the long, blue shadows, my trainers thudding hard against the pavement.

I was out. I was okay. I had seen the monster, but he hadn't seen me. I hoped.

I ran until I got to Aaron's house. He was still in the front garden. He was sitting on the stump of an old tree his parents had removed. I could see the blue frisbee-type thing in his lap. He was struggling to untangle the long rubber band.

Aaron had his head down, concentrating on undoing the knots, and didn't see me at first.

"Aaron—Mr Mortman is a monster!" I cried breathlessly.

"Huh?" He looked up, startled.

"Mr Mortman—he's a monster!" I repeated, panting like a dog. I put my hands on my knees and leaned forward, trying to catch my breath.

"Lucy, what's your problem?" Aaron muttered, returning his attention to the rubber band.

"*Listen to me!*" I screamed impatiently. I didn't sound like myself. I didn't recognize my shrill, panicky voice.

"This thing stinks," Aaron muttered. "It's totally tangled."

"Aaron, *please!*" I pleaded. "I was in the library. I saw him. He changed into a monster. He ate one of his turtles!"

Aaron laughed. "Yum!" he said. "Did you bring *me* one?"

"Aaron, it isn't funny!" I cried, still out of breath. "I—I was so scared. He's a monster. He really is. I thought I was locked in with him. I thought—"

"Tell you what," Aaron said, still picking at the knots in the rubber band. He held the blue plastic disc up to me. "If you can untangle this big knot, I'll let you play with it."

"Aaaaaagh!" I let out an angry scream. "*Why don't you listen to me?*"

"Lucy, give me a break," Aaron said, still holding the disc up to me. "I don't want to talk about monsters now. It's babyish, you know?"

"But, Aaron!"

"Why don't you save that stuff for Randy?" Aaron suggested. He waved the blue disc. "Do you want to help me with this or not?"

"*Not!*" I screamed. Then I added: "You're a *lousy* friend!"

He looked a little surprised.

I didn't wait for him to say anything else. I took off again, heading for home.

I was really angry. What was *his* problem, anyway? You're supposed to take a friend

182

seriously. You're not supposed to think automatically that your friend is just making up a story.

Couldn't Aaron see how frightened and upset I was? Couldn't he see that it wasn't a joke?

He's a total jerk, I decided, as my house finally came into view. I'm never speaking to him again.

I ran up the drive, pulled open the screen door, and burst into the house. "Mum! Dad!" My heart was pounding so hard, my mouth was so dry, my cry was a hoarse whisper.

"Mum—where are you?"

I ran through the house until I found Randy in the study. He was lying on the floor, his face five centimetres from the TV, watching a Bugs Bunny cartoon.

"Where are Mum and Dad?" I cried breathlessly.

He ignored me. Just stared at his cartoon. The colours from the TV danced over his face.

"Randy—where *are* they?" I repeated frantically.

"Grocery shopping," he muttered without turning around.

"But I have to talk to them!" I said. "When did they leave? When will they be back?"

He shrugged without taking his eyes off the screen. "I don't know."

"But, Randy!"

"Leave me alone," he whined. "I'm watching a cartoon."

"But I saw a monster!" I screamed. "A real one!"

His eyes went wide. His mouth dropped open. "A real monster?" he stammered.

"Yes!" I cried.

"Did he follow you home?" Randy asked, turning pale.

"I hope not!" I exclaimed. I wheeled around and ran out of the study. I glanced out of the living room window as I hurried past. No sign of my parents' car.

So I ran up to my room.

I was so upset. So angry and upset.

I took two steps into my room, then stopped.

There in my bed, under the covers, lay a big, hairy monster, its gnarled brown head on my pillow, its gaping, toothless mouth twisted in an evil grin.

I grabbed the top of my dressing table and uttered a loud gasp of shock.

The monster stared at me, one round eye bigger than the other. It didn't move off my pillow.

It uttered a high-pitched giggle.

I mean, I *thought* it giggled. It took me a short while to realize that the giggling was coming from behind me.

I spun around to see Randy just outside the door. When he saw the terrified look on my face, his giggle became a roar of laughter.

"Like it?" he asked, stepping past me into the room and walking up to my bed. "I made it in art class."

"Huh?"

Randy picked up the lumpy brown monster head. As soon as he picked it up, I saw that the hair was brown wool, and that the face was painted on.

"It's papier-mâché," Randy announced proudly. "Good, huh?"

I let out a long sigh and slumped onto the edge of the bed. "Yeah. Great," I muttered unhappily.

"I put the pillows under your covers to make it look like he had a body," Randy continued, grinning. His grin looked a lot like the grin on the monster head.

"Very clever," I said bitterly. "Listen, Randy, I've just had a really scary experience. And I'm really not in the mood for jokes."

His grin grew wider. He tossed the brown monster head at me.

I caught it and held it in my lap. He motioned for me to toss it back, but I didn't.

"Didn't you hear me?" I cried. "I'm very upset. I saw a monster. A real one. In the library."

"You're just embarrassed because my monster head fooled you," Randy said. "You're annoyed because I really scared you."

"Mr Mortman is a monster," I told him, bouncing the monster head on my lap. "I saw him change into a monster. His head grew big, and his eyes popped out, and his mouth twisted open."

"Stop it!" Randy cried, starting to look scared.

"I saw him eat flies," I continued. "Handfuls of flies."

"Flies?" Randy asked. "Yuck!"

"And then I saw him pick up one of his pet

turtles. You know. The ones he keeps in that pan on his desk. I saw him pop it in his mouth and eat it."

Randy shuddered. He stared at me thoughtfully. For a moment, I thought maybe he believed me. But then his expression changed, and he shook his head.

"No way, Lucy. You're just annoyed because I scared you for once. So now you're trying to scare me. But it isn't going to work."

Randy grabbed the monster head from my lap and started out of the door. "I don't believe you about Mr Mortman."

"But it's true!" I protested shrilly.

"I'm missing my cartoons," he said.

Just then, I heard a knock at the front door.

"Mum!" I cried. I leapt off the bed and went tearing to the stairs. I shoved Randy out of my way, and practically flew down the steps, taking them three at a time.

"Mum! Dad—you're home! I have to tell you—"

I froze in front of the screen door.

It wasn't my parents.

It was Mr Mortman.

My first thought was to *run*.

My next thought was to slam the front door.

My next thought was to run back upstairs and hide in my room.

But it was too late to hide. Mr Mortman had already seen me. He was staring at me through the screen door with those beady black eyes, an evil, thin-lipped smile on his pale, round face.

He saw me, I realized.

He saw me spying on him in the library.

He saw me running away.

He knows that I know his secret. He knows that I know he's a monster.

And he's come to get me.

He's come to get rid of me, to make sure his secret is safe.

"Lucy?" he called.

I stared at him through the screen.

I could see in his eyes that he knew it had been me in the library.

The sun had nearly gone down. The sky behind him was sunset-purple. His face looked even paler than usual in the evening light.

"Lucy, hi. It's me," he said.

He was waiting for me to say something. But I was frozen there in panic, trying to decide whether to run or scream. Or both.

Randy had stopped halfway down the stairs. "Who is it?" he asked.

"It's Mr Mortman," I replied softly.

"Oh," said my little brother. He came the rest of the way down, then walked past me on his way back to the study.

"Hi, Mr Mortman," I managed to say, not moving any closer to the door. Then I blurted out, "My parents aren't at home."

I knew instantly that it was a stupid thing to say.

Now the monster knew that Randy and I were here alone.

Why did I say that? I asked myself. *How could I be so stupid?*

"I didn't come to see your parents," Mr Mortman said softly. "I came to see you, Lucy."

He knows! I thought. *He really knows! I'm dead meat!*

I swallowed hard. I didn't know what to say. My eyes searched the front hall for a weapon, something to hit him with when he broke through the screen door and came after me.

Mr Mortman's eyes narrowed. His smile faded.

This is it! I thought.

There was nothing around that I could use to fight him off. A little glass flower vase. That's all I could see. I didn't think it would be too effective against a roaring monster.

"Lucy, I believe this belongs to you," Mr Mortman said. He held up my blue canvas rucksack.

"Huh?"

"I found it at the back of the stacks," Mr Mortman said, his smile returning. "I didn't know who had left it. But I found your name and address on the tag here."

"You—you mean—?" I stammered.

"I always walk home after I close the library, so I thought I'd bring it to you," he said.

Was this a trap?

I studied his face warily. I couldn't tell *what* he was thinking.

I had no choice. I pushed open the screen door, and he handed me the rucksack. "Wow. Thanks," I said. "That was really nice of you."

He straightened the sleeves of his yellow poloneck. "Well, I thought you'd probably want to get started on *Anne of Green Gables* tonight," he said.

"Yeah. Of course," I replied uncertainly.

"I think you must have run out of the library

pretty quickly," Mr Mortman said, staring into my eyes.

"Uh . . . yeah. I had to get home," I told him, glancing back to the study. The cartoon music floated into the hall.

"So you didn't wait around or anything after our appointment?" he asked.

Does he know? I wondered.

Or is he just trying to find out if it was me or not?

"No," I said, trying to keep my voice from shaking. "I ran straight out. I was in a hurry. I—I suppose that's why I forgot my bag."

"Oh, I see," Mr Mortman replied thoughtfully, rubbing his chins.

"Why?" I blurted out.

The question seemed to surprise him. "Oh, it's nothing, really," he said. "I think someone was playing a trick on me. Staying in the library after closing."

"Really?" I asked, opening my eyes wide and trying to sound as innocent as possible. "Why would they do that?"

"To scare me," Mr Mortman answered, chuckling. "Some kids don't have anything better to do than try to scare the kindly old librarian."

But you're *not* a kindly old librarian, I thought. You're a *monster!*

"I got up to look around," Mr Mortman

continued, "and whoever it was had legged it."
He chuckled again.

"I wouldn't want to be locked in there over-night," I said, studying his face, hoping my innocent act was working.

"Neither would I!" he exclaimed. "It's a pretty creepy old building! Sometimes I get so scared from all the strange creaks and groans."

Yeah. Sure! I thought sarcastically.

Behind him, I saw my parents' car turn into the drive. I breathed a silent sigh of relief. Thank *goodness* they were finally home!

"I suppose I'll say good night," Mr Mortman said pleasantly. He turned and watched as my parents rolled past him up the drive, heading for the back of the house.

"Thanks for bringing the bag," I said, eager to go and meet Mum and Dad.

"No problem. See you next week." He hurried away.

I went running through to the kitchen. Mum was just coming in through the kitchen door, carrying a brown grocery bag. "Wasn't that Mr Mortman at the front door?" she asked, surprised.

"Yeah," I answered eagerly. "I'm so glad to see you, Mum. I have to tell you—"

"What did he want?" Mum interrupted.

"He ... uh ... returned my rucksack. I left it at

192

the library. I have to tell you about him, Mum. He—"

"That was really nice of him," Mum said, setting the grocery bag down on the worktop. "How come you forgot it, Lucy?"

"I ran out of there really fast, Mum. You see—"

"Well, that was really nice of Mr Mortman," she interrupted again. She started to remove things from the grocery bag. "He doesn't live in this direction. I think he lives right over on the north side of town."

"Mum, I'm *trying* to tell you something!" I cried impatiently. My hands were clenched into tight fists. My heart was pounding. "Mr Mortman is a monster!"

"Huh?" She turned away from the worktop and stared at me.

"He's a monster, Mum! A real one!" I cried.

"Lucy, Lucy." She shook her head. "You and your monsters."

"Mum!"

"Stop it, Lucy. Stop being silly, now. I hope you were polite to Mr Mortman."

"Mu-um!"

"Enough. Go outside and help your father bring in the rest of the groceries."

So, once again my wonderful parents refused to believe me.

I tried to describe what I had seen from my hiding place in the library. But Mum just shook her head. Dad said I had a great imagination. Even Randy refused to be scared. He told Mum and Dad how he had scared me with his stupid papier-mâché monster head.

I practically begged them to believe me.

But Mum said I was just lazy. She said I was making up the story about Mr Mortman so I could get out of the Reading Rangers course and wouldn't have to read any more books this summer.

When she said that, I got really insulted, of course. I shouted something back. And it ended up with all of us growling and snapping at each other, followed by me storming up to my room.

Slumped unhappily on my bed, I thought hard about my predicament.

I could see that they were never going to believe me.

I had told too many monster stories, played too many monster jokes.

So, I realized, I needed someone else to tell my parents about Mr Mortman. I needed someone else to see Mr Mortman become a monster. I needed someone else to *believe* the truth with me.

Aaron.

If Aaron came along with me and hid in the library and saw Mr Mortman eating flies and turtles with his bulging head—then Aaron could tell my parents.

And they'd believe Aaron.

They had no reason *not* to believe Aaron. He was a serious, no-nonsense type. My most serious, no-nonsense friend.

Aaron was definitely the answer to my problem.

Aaron would finally make my parents realize the truth about Mr Mortman.

I phoned him immediately.

I told him I needed him to come and hide in the library and spy on Mr Mortman with me.

"When?" he asked. "At your next Reading Rangers meeting?"

"No. I can't wait a whole week," I said, whispering into the phone, even though my parents were downstairs and there was no one around. "How about tomorrow afternoon? Just before closing time. Around five."

"It's too stupid," Aaron insisted. "I don't think I want to."

"I'll *pay* you!" I blurted out.

"How much?" he asked.

What a friend!

"Five dollars," I said reluctantly. I never save much of my pocket money. I wondered if I still had five dollars in my drawer.

"Well, okay," Aaron agreed. "Five dollars. In advance."

"And you'll hide with me and then tell my parents everything you see?" I asked.

"Yeah. Okay. But I still think it's pretty stupid." He was silent for a moment. "And what if we get caught?" he asked after a while.

"We'll be careful," I said, feeling a little chill of fear.

I spent most of the next day hanging around,
teasing Randy. I couldn't wait for the afternoon
to come round.

I was so excited. And nervous.

I had it all worked out. Aaron and I would
sneak into the main reading room without
Mr Mortman knowing anyone had come in.
We'd hide in the dark shelves, just as I had
done.

Then, when the librarian turned off the lights
and closed up the library, we'd sneak up the
aisle, keeping in the shadows, and watch him
become a monster.

We wouldn't run out the way I had done.
That was far too risky. We would go back to our
hiding places in the low shelves and wait for
Mr Mortman to leave. Once he was gone, Aaron
and I would let ourselves out of the library and
hurry to my house to tell my parents what we
had seen.

Easy. Nothing to it, I kept telling myself.

But I was so nervous, so eager to get it over with, I arrived at Aaron's house an hour early. I rang the bell.

No answer.

I rang it again.

Finally, after a long wait, Aaron's teenage brother, Burt, pulled open the door. He had on blue denim shorts and no shirt. "Hi," he said, scratching his chest. "You looking for Aaron?"

"Yeah." I nodded.

"He isn't here."

"Huh?" I practically fell off the porch. "Where is he? I mean, when will he be back?"

"Don't know. He went to the dentist," Burt said, gazing past me to the street.

"He did?"

"Yeah. He had an appointment. With the orthodontist. He's getting a brace. Didn't he tell you?"

"No," I said glumly. I could feel my heart sink to my knees. "I was supposed to meet him."

"Suppose he forgot," Burt said with a shrug. "You know Aaron. He never remembers things like that."

"Well. Thanks," I muttered unhappily. I said goodbye and trudged back down to the pavement.

That dirty traitor.

I felt really betrayed.

I had waited all day. I was so *psyched up* for spying on Mr Mortman.

I had counted on Aaron. And all the while, he had a stupid orthodontist appointment.

"I hope your brace really hurts!" I shouted out loud.

I kicked a small stone across the pavement. I felt like kicking a *lot* of stones. I felt like kicking Aaron.

I turned and headed for home, thinking all kinds of ugly thoughts. I was at the bottom of my drive when an idea popped into my head.

I didn't need Aaron, I suddenly realized.

I had a camera.

My parents had given me a really good camera last Christmas.

If I sneaked into the library with the camera and took a few snapshots of Mr Mortman after he became a monster, the photos would be all the proof I needed.

My parents would *have* to believe actual colour photographs.

Forgetting my disappointment about Aaron, I hurried up to my room and pulled the camera off the shelf. It already had film in it. I had taken a lot of photos at Randy's birthday party just before school had finished for the summer.

I examined it carefully. There were still eight or nine shots left on the roll.

That should be plenty to capture Mr Mortman at his ugliest.

I glanced at the clock on my desk. It was still early. Just after four-thirty. I had half an hour before the library closed.

"This has *got* to work," I said out loud, crossing my fingers on both hands.

Then I strapped the camera around my neck and headed for the library.

I entered the library silently and crept to the doorway of the main reading room. My plan was to sneak into the low shelf where I had hidden before. But I quickly saw that it wasn't going to be as easy as I thought.

The library was very crowded. There were several kids in the children's book section. There were people thumbing through the magazines. One of the microfiche machines was being used against one wall. And several aisles, including the one with my special hiding place, had people in them, browsing and searching the shelves.

I'll just have to hang around until they've all gone, I decided, turning and pretending to search on one of the back shelves.

I could see Mr Mortman standing behind his desk. He was checking out a pile of books for a young woman, opening the covers, stamping the card, then slamming the covers shut.

It was nearly five o'clock. Just about closing time.

I crept along the back wall, searching for another hiding place. Near the corner, I spotted a large wooden càbinet. I recognized it as I stepped behind it and lowered myself from view. It was the long, tall cabinet that held the card catalogue.

It will hide me quite nicely, I thought.

I hunched down behind the old cabinet and waited. Time dragged by. Every second seemed like an hour.

At five-fifteen, Mr Mortman was still checking out books for people. He announced closing time, but some of the magazine readers seemed very reluctant to leave.

I felt myself getting more and more nervous. My hands were ice cold. The camera suddenly seemed to weigh a thousand pounds, like a dead weight around my neck. I removed it and dropped it to my lap.

It will be worth it, I kept repeating to myself.

It will be worth it if I get a good, clear shot of the monster.

I leaned against the back of the cabinet and waited, my hand gripping the camera in my lap.

Finally, the room emptied out.

I climbed to my knees, suddenly very alert, as I heard the librarian go to lock the front door. A few seconds later, I heard him return to his desk.

I stood up and peered around the side of the cabinet. He was busily shuffling papers, straightening his desk for the night.

In a few minutes, I hoped, it would be feeding time.

Monster time.

Taking a deep breath, I gripped the camera tightly in one hand and, feeling my heart start to pound, began to make my way silently towards Mr Mortman's desk at the front of the room.

Everything seemed to be taking so long today.

Was time really in slow motion? Or did everything seem so slow because my pulse was racing so fast?

I was so eager to get my proof—and get out of there!

But Mr Mortman was certainly taking his time. He shuffled through a pile of papers, reading some of them, folding some of them in half, and tossing them in the wastepaper basket beside his desk.

He hummed to himself as he read through the entire pile. Finally, he got to the bottom of the pile and tossed the last sheet away.

Now! I thought. *Now you'll start your monster routine, won't you, Mr Mortman!*

But no.

He lifted a pile of books from his desk and carried them to the shelves. Humming loudly, he started returning the books to their places.

I pressed myself into the shadows, hoping he wouldn't come to my row. I was near the far wall in front of the row of microfiche machines.

Please, let's get on with it! I begged silently.

But when he'd finished with the first pile, Mr Mortman returned to his desk and hoisted up another pile of books to replace.

I'm going to be late for dinner, I realized with a growing sense of dread. My parents are going to *kill* me!

The thought made me chuckle. Here I was locked inside this creepy old library with a monster, and I was worried about getting scolded for being late for dinner!

I could hear Mr Mortman, but I couldn't see him. He was somewhere among the rows of shelves, replacing books.

Suddenly his humming grew louder.

I realized he was in the next aisle. I could see him over the tops of the books on the shelf to my right.

And that meant *he* could see *me*!

Gripped with panic, I ducked and dropped to the floor.

Had he heard me? Had he seen me?

I didn't move. I didn't breathe.

He continued to hum to himself. The sound grew fainter as he moved in the other direction.

Letting out a silent sigh of relief, I climbed back to my feet. Gripping the camera tightly in my right hand, I peered around the side of the shelf.

I heard his shoes shuffling along the floor. He reappeared, his bald head shiny in the late afternoon sunlight from the window, and made his way slowly to his desk.

The clock on the wall ticked noisily.

My hand gripping the camera was cold and clammy.

Watching him shuffle things around inside his desk drawer, I suddenly lost my nerve.

This is stupid, I thought. A really bad idea.

I'm going to get caught.

As soon as I step out to take the picture, he'll see me.

He'll chase after me. He won't let me get out of the library with this camera.

He won't let me get out of here *alive*.

Turn and run! a voice inside my head commanded.

Quick, while you have the chance—turn and run!

Then another voice interrupted that one. *He isn't going to turn into a monster tonight, Lucy,* the voice said. *You're wasting your time. You're getting yourself all nervous and scared for no reason.*

My mind was spinning, whirring with voices and frightening thoughts. I leaned hard against the wooden shelf, steadying myself. I closed my eyes for a moment, trying to clear my head.

How many shots can you take? A voice in my head asked. *Can you shoot off three or four before he realizes what is happening?*

You only need one good shot, another voice told me. *One good clear shot will be the proof you need.*

You'd better hope he's humming very loudly, another voice said. *Otherwise, he'll hear your camera shutter click.*

Turn and run! another voice repeated. *Turn and run!*

You only need one good shot.

Don't let him hear your shutter click.

I stepped forward and peered round the shelf.

Mr Mortman, humming happily away, was reaching for the fly jar.

Yes! I cried silently. *Finally.*

"Dinnertime, my timid friends," I heard him say in a pleasant singsong. And as he started to unscrew the jar lid, his head began to grow.

His eyes bulged. His mouth twisted open and enlarged.

In a few seconds, his monstrous head was bobbing above his shirt. His snakelike tongue flicked out of his black mouth as he removed the jar lid and pulled out a handful of flies.

"Dinnertime, my timid friends!"

Picture time! I thought, gathering my courage.

I raised the camera to my eye with a trembling hand. I gripped it tightly with both hands to keep it from shaking.

Then, holding my breath, I leaned as far forward as I could.

Mr Mortman was downing his first handful of flies, chewing noisily, humming as he chewed.

I struggled to centre him in the viewfinder.

I was so nervous, the camera was shaking all over the place!

I'm so glad he's humming, I thought, raising my finger to the shutter button.

He won't hear the camera click.

I'll be able to take more than one shot.

Okay. Okay ...

He was still enjoying his first batch of tender flies.

Now! I told myself.

I was about to push the button—when Mr Mortman suddenly turned away.

With a gasp, I stopped myself just in time.

My pulse was pounding at my temples so hard, I could barely see straight.

What was he doing?

He was reaching for another jar. He put it down on his desk and unscrewed the lid.

I raised the camera again and squinted at him through the viewfinder.

What did he have in this jar? Something was

fluttering in there. It took me a while to realize they were moths. White moths.

He closed his fist around one and shoved it hungrily into his mouth. Another moth fluttered out of the jar before he could close the lid.

Mr Mortman's eyes bulged like toadstools growing out of his balloonlike head. His mouth twisted and coiled as he chewed the moth.

Taking another deep breath and holding it, I leaned forward as far as I could, steadied the camera in front of my eye—and snapped the shutter.

The FLASH!

I had forgotten about the flash!

I was so worried about the click of the shutter I
had totally forgotten that my camera had
automatic flash!

The instant flash of white light made Mr
Mortman cry out angrily. Startled, he raised his
hands to cover his bulging eyes.

I stood frozen in the aisle, frozen by careless-
ness, frozen by my stupidity!

"*Who's* there?" he growled, still covering his
eyes.

I realized he hadn't seen me yet. Those big
eyes must have been very sensitive to light. The
flash had momentarily blinded him.

He let out a monstrous roar that echoed off the
four walls of the vast room.

Somehow I revived my senses enough to pull
myself back, out of view.

"Who's there?" he repeated, his voice a

rasping snarl. "You won't get away!"

I saw him lumbering in my direction. As he lurched towards me, his body swayed awkwardly, as if his eyes were still blinded.

I gaped in horror as he approached.

He seemed steadier with each step. His bulging eyes searched the rows of shelves. He was breathing hard, each breath a furious growl.

"Who's there? Who's there?"

Get going! I told myself, still gripping the camera in both hands. *Get going! What are you waiting for?*

"You won't get away!" the monster cried.

Oh, yes, I will!

He was three rows away, his eyes peering down the dark aisles. Searching. Searching.

He hadn't seen me, I knew. The light of the flash had startled him, then blinded him.

He didn't know it was me.

Now all I had to do was run. All I had to do was get out of there with the proof safely in my hands.

So what was I waiting for?

He lumbered closer. He was only a row away.

Run! I ordered my paralyzed legs. *Run! Don't just stand there!*

I spun round, clumsily bumping into a shelf of books. Several books toppled to the floor.

Run! Don't stop!

It was taking me so long to move. I was weighed down by my fear.

Run, Lucy! He's right behind you!

Finally, my legs started to cooperate.

Holding the camera in one hand, I began to run through the dark aisle towards the back of the room.

"You won't get away!" the monster bellowed from the next aisle. "I hear you! I know where you are!"

Uttering an animal cry of terror, I ran blindly to the end of the aisle, turned towards the doorway—and crashed into a low book trolley.

The trolley toppled over as I fell on top of it.

I landed hard on my stomach and knees. The camera bounced from my hand and slid across the floor.

"I've got you now!" the monster growled, moving quickly from the next aisle.

I scrambled to get up, but my leg was caught in the trolley.

The monster lumbered towards me, panting loudly.

Once again, my fear tried to paralyse me. I tried to push myself up with both hands, but my body felt as if it weighed a thousand pounds.

I'm dead meat! I thought.

Finally, I pushed myself up and freed myself from the trolley.

Dead meat. Dead meat.

The panting, growling monster was only a few metres away now, lurching out of a row of shelves.

I grabbed the camera and stumbled to the door, my knee throbbing, my head whirring.

I'll never make it. Never.

And then I heard the loud electronic ringing.

At first, I thought it was an alarm.

But then I realized it was the telephone.

I pulled myself into the doorway and turned.

The monster hesitated at the end of the aisle. His bulbous, black eyes floated up above his face. His gaping mouth, drooling green liquid, twisted into an O of surprise.

He stopped short, startled by the sudden interruption.

Saved by the bell! I thought happily. I pulled open the heavy front door and burst out to freedom.

I ran for two blocks, my trainers slapping the pavement, my heart refusing to slow its frantic beat. I closed my eyes as I ran, enjoying the feel of the warm, fresh air on my face, the warmth of the late afternoon sun, the sweep of my hair flying behind me as I ran. Feeling *free*. Free and safe!

When I opened my eyes and slowed my pace, I realized that I was gripping the camera so tightly, my hands hurt.

My proof. I had my proof.

One snapshot. One snapshot that nearly cost me my life. But I had it in the camera, my proof that Mr Mortman was a monster.

"I have to get it developed," I said out loud. "Fast."

I jogged the rest of the way home, cradling the camera under my arm.

As my house came into view, I had a chilling

feeling that Mr Mortman would be waiting there. That he would be waiting beside the front porch, waiting to grab the camera from me, to rob me of my proof.

I hesitated at the bottom of the drive.

No one there.

Was he hiding in the bushes? Around the side of the house?

I walked up the front lawn slowly. *You're being stupid*, I scolded myself. *How could Mr Mortman get here before you?*

Besides, I wasn't even sure he had recognized me.

The lights were out in the library. The room was dark. The closest he had come was the aisle next to mine. And he was blinded for a long while by the camera flash.

I started to breathe a little easier. Yes, it was possible that the librarian didn't know who he was chasing. It was possible that he never got a good look at me at all.

My dad's car pulled up the drive as I reached the front porch. I went tearing after him, running around the side of the house to the back.

"Dad! Hi!" I called as he climbed out of the car.

"Hey, how's it going?" he asked. His suit was rumpled. His hair was dishevelled. He looked tired.

"Dad, can we get this film developed—straight away?" I demanded, shoving the camera towards him.

"Whoa!" he cried. "I've just got home. Let's talk about it at dinner, okay?"

"No, Dad—really!" I insisted. "I have to get this developed. There's something very important on it."

He walked past me towards the house, his shoes crunching over the gravel drive.

I followed right behind, still holding my camera up high. "Please, Dad? It's really important. Really really important!"

He turned, chuckling. "What have you got? A picture of that boy who's moved in across the street?"

"No," I replied angrily. "I'm serious, Dad. Can't you take me to the shopping centre? There's that one-hour developing place there."

"What's so important?" he asked, his smile fading. He ran a hand over his head, smoothing down his thick, black hair.

I had the urge to tell him I had a photo of the monster in there. But I stopped myself.

I knew he wouldn't believe me. I knew he wouldn't take me seriously.

And then he wouldn't drive me to the shopping centre to get my film developed. No way.

"I'll show it to you when it's developed," I said.

He held open the screen door. We walked into the kitchen. Dad sniffed the air a couple of times, expecting the aroma of cooking food.

Mum came bursting in from the hall to greet us. "Don't sniff," she told my dad. "There's nothing cooking. We're eating out tonight."

"Great!" I cried. "Can we eat at the shopping centre? At that Chinese restaurant you like?" I turned to my dad. "Please? Please? Then I could get my film developed while we eat."

"I could go for Chinese food," Mum said, thoughtfully. Then she turned her gaze on me. "Why so eager to get your film developed?"

"It's a secret," Dad said before I could reply. "She won't tell."

I couldn't hold it any longer. "It's a picture I snapped of Mr Mortman," I told her excitedly. "It's my proof that he's a monster."

Mum rolled her eyes. Dad shook his head.

"It's proof!" I insisted. "Maybe when you see the photo, you'll finally believe me."

"You're right," Dad said sarcastically. "I'll believe it when I see it."

"Randy! Hurry downstairs," Mum shouted into the hallway. "We're going to the shopping centre for Chinese food!"

"Aw, do we *have* to have Chinese food?" my brother called down unhappily. His standard reply.

"I'll get you the plain *lo mein* noodles you

like," Mum called up to him. "Just hurry. We're all hungry."

I pushed the button on my camera to rewind the roll of film. "I'm going to drop this at the one-hour developing place before dinner," I told them. "Then we can pick it up after dinner."

"No monster talk at dinner tonight—promise?" Mum said sternly. "I don't want you scaring your brother."

"Promise," I said, pulling the film roll out of the camera, squeezing it between my fingers.

After dinner, I told myself, *I won't have to* talk *about monsters—I'll show you one!*

Dinner seemed to take forever.

Randy didn't stop complaining the whole time. He said his noodles tasted funny. He said the spareribs were too greasy, and the soup was too hot. He spilled his glass of water all over the table.

I barely paid any attention to what anyone said. I was thinking about my snapshot. I couldn't wait to see it—and to show it to Mum and Dad.

I could just imagine the looks on their faces when they saw that I was right, that I hadn't been making it up—that Mr Mortman really was a monster.

I imagined both my parents apologizing to me, promising they'd never doubt me again.

"I feel so bad," I imagined my dad saying, "I'm going to buy you that computer you've been asking for."

"And a new bike," I imagined Mum saying. "Please forgive us for doubting you."

"And I'm sorry, too," I imagined Randy saying. "I know I've been a real jerk."

"And you can stay up till midnight every night from now on, even on school nights," I imagined Dad saying.

Suddenly, my mum's voice broke into my daydreams. "Lucy, I don't think you heard a word I said," she scolded.

"No . . . I . . . uh . . . was thinking about something," I admitted. I picked up my chopsticks and raised a chunk of rice to my mouth.

"She was thinking about *monsters*!" Randy cried, raising both hands up over the table, curling his fingers as if he were a monster about to attack me.

"No monster talk!" Mum insisted sharply.

"Don't look at me!" I cried. "He said it—not me!" I pointed an accusing finger at Randy.

"Just finish your dinner," Dad said quietly. He had sparerib grease all over his chin.

Finally, we were opening our fortune cookies. Mine said something about waiting for sunshine when the clouds part. I never get those fortunes.

Dad paid the bill. Randy nearly spilled another glass of water as we were standing up. I went running out of the restaurant. I was so excited, so eager, I couldn't wait another second.

The little photo shop was on the upper level. I leapt onto the escalator, grabbed the rail, and travelled to the top. Then I tore into the shop, up to the counter, and called breathlessly to the young woman at the developing machine, "Are my photos ready yet?"

She turned, startled by my loud voice. "I think so. What's your name?"

I told her. She walked over to a rack of yellow envelopes and began slowly shuffling through them.

I tapped my fingers nervously on the counter, staring at the stack of yellow envelopes. *Couldn't she hurry it up a little?*

She shuffled all the way through the stack, then turned back to me. "What did you say your name was again?"

Trying not to sound too exasperated, I told her my name again. I leaned eagerly on the counter, my heart pounding, and stared at her as she began once again to shuffle through the yellow envelopes, moving her lips as she read the names.

Finally, she pulled one out and handed it to me.

I grabbed it and started to tear it open.

"That comes to fourteen dollars," she said.

I realized I didn't have any money. "I'll have

to get my dad," I told her, not letting go of the precious package.

I turned, and Dad appeared in the doorway. Mum and Randy waited outside.

He paid.

I carried the envelope of photos out of the shop. My hands were shaking as I pulled it open and removed the snapshots.

"Lucy, calm down," Mum said, sounding worried.

I stared down at the snapshots. All photos of Randy's birthday party.

I sifted through them quickly, staring at the grinning faces of Randy's stupid friends.

Where is it? Where is it? Where is it?

Of course, it was the very last photo, the one on the bottom of the pile.

"Here it is!" I cried.

Mum and Dad leaned forward to see over my shoulder.

The other photos fell from my hand and scattered over the floor as I raised the photo to my face—

—and gasped.

The photo was clear and sharp.

Mr Mortman's large desk stood in the centre in a burst of bright light. I could see papers on the desk, the pan of turtles at the far corner, a low pile of books.

Behind the desk, I could see the top of Mr Mortman's tall wooden stool. And behind the stool, the shelves were in clear focus, even the glass jar of flies on the lower shelf.

But there was no monster.

No Mr Mortman.

No one.

No one in the photograph at all.

"He—he was standing right there!" I cried. "Beside the desk!"

"The room looks empty," Dad said, staring down over my shoulder at the photo in my quivering hand.

"There's no one there," Mum said, turning her gaze on me.

"He was there," I insisted, unable to take my eyes off the photo. "Right there." I pointed to where the monster had stood.

Randy laughed. "Let me see." He pulled the photo from my hand and examined it. "I see him!" he declared. "He's invisible!"

"It isn't funny," I said weakly. I pulled the photo away from him. I sighed unhappily. I felt so bad. I wanted to sink into a hole in the floor and never come out.

"He's invisible!" Randy repeated gleefully, enjoying his own joke.

Mum and Dad were staring at me, looks of concern on their faces.

"Don't you see?" I cried, waving the photo in one hand. "Don't you see? This *proves* it! This proves he's a monster. He doesn't show up in photographs!"

Dad shook his head and frowned. "Lucy, haven't you carried this joke far enough?"

Mum put a hand on my shoulder. "I'm starting to get worried about you," she said softly. "I think you're really starting to believe in your own monster joke."

"Can we get some ice cream?" asked Randy.

"I can't believe we're doing this," Aaron complained.

"Just shut up. You *owe* me one!" I snapped.

It was the next evening. We were crouched

down, hiding behind the low hedge at the side of the library.

It was a crisp, cool day. The sun was already lowering itself behind the trees. The shadows stretched long and blue over the library lawn.

"I owe you one?" Aaron protested. "Are you crazy?"

"You owe me one," I repeated. "You were supposed to come to the library with me yesterday, remember? You let me down."

He brushed an insect off his freckled nose. "Can I help it if I had an orthodontist appointment?" He sounded funny. His words were coming out all sticky. He wasn't used to his new brace yet.

"Yes," I insisted. "I counted on you, and you let me down—and you got me into all kinds of trouble."

"What kind of trouble?" He dropped to the ground and sat cross-legged, keeping his head low behind the hedge.

"My parents said I'm never allowed to mention Mr Mortman again, or the fact that he's a monster," I told him.

"Good," Aaron said.

"Not good. It means I really need you, Aaron. I need you to see that I'm telling the truth, and tell my parents." My voice broke. "They think I'm crazy. They really do!"

He started to reply, but he could see I was really upset. So he stopped himself.

A cool breeze swept past, making the trees all seem to whisper at us.

I kept my eyes trained on the library door. It was five-twenty. Past closing time. Mr Mortman should be coming out any second.

"So we're going to follow Mr Mortman home?" Aaron asked, scratching the back of his neck. "And spy on him at his house? Why don't we just watch him through the library window?"

"The window is too high," I replied. "We have to follow him. He told me he walks home every evening. I want you to see him turn into a monster," I said, staring straight ahead over the top of the bush. "I want you to believe me."

"What if I just *say* I believe you?" Aaron asked, grinning. "Then could we just go home?"

"Ssshhh!" I pressed a hand over Aaron's mouth.

The library door was opening. Mr Mortman appeared on the front steps.

Aaron and I ducked down lower.

I peered through the branches of the hedge. The librarian turned to lock the front door. He was wearing a red-and-white-striped short-sleeved sports shirt and baggy grey trousers. He had a red baseball cap on his bald head.

"Stay far behind," I whispered to Aaron. "Don't let him see you."

"Good advice," Aaron said sarcastically.

We both shifted onto our knees and waited for Mr Mortman to head down the pavement. He hesitated on the steps, replacing the keys in his trouser pocket. Then, humming to himself, he walked down the drive and turned away from us.

"What's he humming about?" Aaron whispered.

"He always hums," I whispered back. Mr Mortman was more than half a block away. "Let's go," I said, climbing quickly to my feet.

Keeping in the shadows of the trees and shrubs, I began following the librarian. Aaron followed just behind me.

"Do you know where he lives?" Aaron asked.

I turned back to him, frowning. "If I knew where he lived, we wouldn't have to follow him— would we!"

"Oh. Right."

Following someone was a lot harder than I'd thought. We had to cut through front gardens. Some of them had barking dogs. Some had lawn sprinklers going. Some had thick hedges we somehow had to duck through.

At every street corner, Mr Mortman would stop and look both ways for oncoming cars. Each time, I was certain he was going to look over his shoulder, too, and see Aaron and me creeping along behind him.

225

He lived farther from the library than I had realized. After several blocks, the houses ended, and a bare, flat field spread in front of us.

Mr Mortman cut through the field, walking quickly, swinging his stubby arms rhythmically with each step. We had no choice but to follow him across the field. There were no hiding places. No shrubs to duck behind. No hedges to shield us.

We were completely out in the open. We just had to pray that he didn't turn around in the middle of the field and see us.

A block of small, older houses stood beyond the field. Most of the houses were brick, set close to the street on tiny front gardens.

Mr Mortman turned onto a block of these houses. Aaron and I crouched behind a postbox and watched him walk up to a house near the middle of the block. He stepped onto the small front step, and fiddled in his pocket for the keys.

"We're here," I whispered to Aaron. "We made it."

"My friend Ralph lives on this block, I think," Aaron said.

"Who cares?" I snapped. "Keep your mind on the job, okay?"

We waited until Mr Mortman had disappeared through the front door of his house, then crept closer.

His house was white weatherboard, badly in need of a paint job. He had a small rectangle of a front garden, with recently cut grass bordered by a single row of tall, yellow tiger lilies.

Aaron and I made our way quickly to the side of the house where there was a narrow strip of grass that led to the back. The window near the front of the house was high enough for us to stand under and not be seen.

A light came on in the window. "That must be his living room," I whispered.

Aaron had a frightened expression. His freckles seemed a lot paler than usual. "I don't like this," he said.

"The hard part was following him," I assured Aaron. "This part is easy. We just watch him through the window."

"But the window is too high," Aaron pointed out. "We can't see anything."

He was right. Staring up from beneath the window, all I could see was the living room ceiling.

"We'll have to stand on something," I said.

"Huh? What?"

I could see Aaron was going to be no help. He was so frightened, his nose was twitching like a bunny rabbit's. I decided if I could keep him busy, maybe I could keep him from totally freaking out and running away.

"Go round the back. See if there's a ladder or something," I whispered, motioning towards the back of the house.

Another light came on, this one in a back window. Probably the kitchen, I thought. It was also too high to see into.

"Wait. What about that?" Aaron asked. I followed his gaze to a wheelbarrow, tilted against the side of the house.

"Yeah. Maybe," I said. "Bring it over. I'll try to stand on it."

Keeping his head and shoulders bent low, Aaron scampered over to the wheelbarrow. He lifted it away from the house by the handles, then pushed it under the front window.

"Hold it steady," I said.

He grabbed the wooden handles, gazing up at me fearfully. "You sure about this?"

"I'll give it a try," I said, glancing up at the high window.

Holding onto Aaron's shoulder, I gave myself a boost onto the wheelbarrow. He held on firmly to the handles as I struggled to find my balance inside the metal basket part.

"It—it's kind of tilty," I whispered, pressing one hand against the side of the house to steady myself.

"I'm doing the best I can," Aaron grumbled.

"There. I think I can stand," I said. I wasn't very high off the ground, but I wasn't at all comfortable. A wheelbarrow is a difficult thing to stand on.

Somewhere down the road a dog barked. I hoped he wasn't barking because of Aaron and me.

Another dog, closer to us, quickly joined in, and it became a barking conversation.

"Are you high enough? Can you see anything?" Aaron asked.

One hand still pressed against the side of the house, I raised my head and peered into the house through the bottom of the window.

"Yeah. I can see a bit," I called down. "There's a big aquarium in front of the window, but I can see most of the living room."

And just as I said that, Mr Mortman's face loomed inches from mine.

He was staring right at me!

I gasped and lost my balance.

I toppled to the ground, knocking over the wheelbarrow, landing hard on my knees and elbows. "Ow!"

"What happened?" Aaron cried, alarmed.

"He saw me!" I choked out, waiting for the pain to stop throbbing.

"Huh?" Aaron's mouth dropped open.

We both gazed up at the window. I expected to see Mr Mortman staring down at us.

But no. No sign of him.

I climbed quickly to my feet. "Maybe he was looking at his aquarium," I whispered, motioning for Aaron to set up the wheelbarrow. "Maybe he didn't see me."

"Wh-what are you going to do?" Aaron stammered.

"Get back up, of course," I told him. My legs were shaking as I climbed back onto the wheelbarrow. I grabbed the window ledge and pulled myself up.

The sun had nearly gone down. The darkness outside made it easier to see inside the house. And, I hoped, harder for Mr Mortman to see out.

I didn't have the best view in the world, I quickly realized. The aquarium, crowded with colourful tropical fish, blocked my view of most of the room.

If only I were a little higher, I thought, I could see over it. But if I *had* been higher, I realized, Mr Mortman would have seen me.

"What's he doing?" Aaron asked in a trembling whisper.

"Nothing. He's . . . wait!"

Mr Mortman was staring down at the fish. He stood only a few feet from me, on the other side of the aquarium.

I froze, pressing my hands against the side of the house.

He gazed down into his aquarium, and a smile formed on his pudgy face. He had removed the red baseball cap. His bald head looked yellow in the living room lamplight.

His mouth moved. He was saying something to the tropical fish in the aquarium. I couldn't hear him through the glass.

Then, as he smiled down at his fish, he began to change.

"He's doing it," I whispered to Aaron. "He's turning into a monster."

As I watched Mr Mortman's head inflate and his eyes bulge out, I was filled with all kinds of strange feelings. I was terrified. And I was fascinated. It was exciting to be so close, inches away from a real monster.

And I felt so happy and relieved that Aaron would finally see for himself that I was telling the truth.

Then, as Mr Mortman's mouth grew wider and began to gyrate, a twisting black hole on his swollen, yellow face, fear overtook me. I froze there, my face pressed against the window, not blinking, not moving.

I stared as he reached a hand into the aquarium.

His fat fingers wrapped around a slender blue fish. He pulled it up and flipped it into his mouth. I could see long, yellow teeth inside the enormous mouth, biting down, chewing the wriggling fish.

Then, as I gaped in growing terror, Mr Mortman pulled a black snail off the side of the aquarium glass. Holding its shell between his fingertips, he stuffed the snail into his mouth. His teeth crunched down hard on the shell, cracking it—a crack so loud, I could hear it through the window glass.

My stomach churned. I felt sick.

He swallowed the snail, then reached to pull another one off the aquarium glass.

"I think I'm going to throw up my lunch," I whispered down to Aaron.

Aaron.

I had forgotten all about him.

I was so fascinated by the monster, so excited, so terrified to watch him close up, I had forgotten the whole purpose of being here.

"Aaron, help me down," I whispered. "Quick."

Still staring through the window, I reached a hand down for Aaron to take it.

"Aaron—hurry! Help me down so you can climb up here. You have to see this! You have to see the monster!"

He didn't reply.

"Aaron? Aaron?"

I lowered my eyes from the window.

Aaron had disappeared.

I felt a stab of panic in my chest.

My whole body convulsed in a tremor of cold fear.

Where was he?

Had he run away?

Was Aaron so frightened that he just ran off without telling me?

Or had something happened to him? Something really bad?

"Aaron? Aaron?" In my panic, I forgot that I was centimetres away from a monster, and started to shout. "Aaron? Where *are* you?"

"Ssh," I heard a whisper from the back of the house. Aaron appeared, making his way quickly towards me along the narrow strip of grass. "I'm right here, Lucy."

"Huh? Where'd you go?"

He pointed to the back of the house. "I thought maybe I could find a ladder or something. You know. So I could see, too."

"You scared me half to death!" I cried.

I returned my glance to the window. Mr Mortman was sucking a slithering eel into his mouth like a strand of spaghetti.

"Quick, Aaron—help me down," I instructed, still feeling shaken from the scare of his disappearance. "You have to see this. You have to. Before he changes back."

"He—he's really a monster?" Aaron's mouth dropped open. "You're not joking?"

"Just get up here!" I cried impatiently.

But as I tried to lower myself to the ground, the wheelbarrow slid out from under me.

It toppled onto its side, the handles scraping the side of the house.

My hands shot up to grab the windowsill. I missed and fell heavily on top of the wheelbarrow. "Ow!" I cried out as sharp pain cut through my side.

Glancing up, I saw the monster's startled face, goggling down at me through the glass.

I scrambled to get up. But the throbbing pain in my side took my breath away.

"Aaron—help me!"

But he was already running to the street, his trainers scraping the grass, his arms stretched straight out in front of him as if trying to grab onto safety.

Ignoring the pain in my side, I scrambled to my feet.

I took an unsteady step, then another. I shook my head, trying to shake away my dizziness.

Then I sucked in a deep breath and started to run, following Aaron towards the street.

I had gone about four or five steps when I felt Mr Mortman's surprisingly strong hands grab my shoulders from behind.

I tried to scream, but no sound came out.

He held firmly onto my shoulders. I could feel his hot, clammy hands through my T-shirt.

I tried to pull away, but he was too strong.

He spun round.

His face was back to normal.

He squinted at me with those little black eyes, as if he couldn't believe what he was seeing. "Lucy!" he exclaimed in his scratchy voice.

He let go of my shoulders and stepped back.

I was panting loudly. I was so frightened, my chest felt about to explode.

How had he changed back from his monster form so quickly?

What was he going to do to me?

"Lucy, good heavens. I thought you were a burglar," he said, shaking his head. He removed a white handkerchief from his back pocket and wiped his perspiring forehead.

"S-sorry," I stammered. My voice came out in a choked whisper.

He rolled up the handkerchief between his fat hands and jammed it back into his pocket. "What are you doing here?"

"Well . . ." My heart was pounding so hard, I could feel the blood pulsing in my temples. My side still ached from where I had fallen on the wheelbarrow.

I struggled to clear my mind. I had to think of an answer to his question. I *had* to.

"Well . . ." I started again, thinking desperately. "I . . . uh . . . came to tell you that I'll . . . uh . . . be a little late for my Reading Rangers appointment tomorrow."

He narrowed his eyes and stared at me thoughtfully. "But why were you looking through my window?" he demanded.

"Well . . . I just . . ."

Think, Lucy—think!

"I didn't know if you were at home or not. I was just trying to see if you were there. I mean. So I could tell you. About the appointment tomorrow."

Staring into his face, trying to sound sincere, I took a step back, in case I had to make a run for it.

Did he believe me?

Was he buying it?

I couldn't tell. He continued to stare at me thoughtfully.

He rubbed his chins. "You really didn't have to come all the way out here," he said softly. "Did you ride your bike?" His eyes darted over the small front lawn.

"No. I ... uh ... walked. I like to walk," I replied awkwardly.

"It's getting dark," he said. "Maybe you should phone your mum or dad to come and pick you up. Why don't you come inside and use the phone?"

Come inside?

Come inside the monster's house?

No way!

"Uh . . . no thanks, Mr Mortman," I said, taking another step backwards towards the street. "My parents don't mind if I walk home. It isn't that far. Really."

"No. I insist," he said, an odd grin starting across his molelike face. He motioned towards the house. "Come on in, Lucy. The phone is in the living room," he urged. "Come on. I won't bite."

I shuddered.

I'd just seen him bite snails. And eels.

There was no way I was going into that house. I knew that if I went in, chances are I'd never come out.

"I—I've got to go," I said, giving him a wave of

one hand. I could feel the fear creeping up my back, running over my body. I knew if I didn't get away from there—*that moment*—I'd be frozen by my terror, unable to escape.

"Lucy—" Mr Mortman insisted.

"No. Really. Bye, Mr Mortman." I waved again, turned, and started jogging to the street.

"You really shouldn't have come all this way!" he called after me in his high, scratchy voice. "Really. You shouldn't have!"

I know! I thought. *I know I shouldn't have.*

I trotted along the street, turned the corner, and continued down the next street.

Was I really getting away?

Was he really letting me go?

I couldn't believe he'd bought my pathetic excuse.

Why was he letting me get away?

I slowed to a walk. My side still ached. I suddenly had a throbbing headache.

Night had fallen. Passing cars had their headlights on. A slender trail of dark cloud drifted over a pale half-moon still low in the purple-grey sky.

I was about to cross the street onto the broad, empty field when hands grabbed my shoulders again.

I cried out, more of a *yelp* than a scream, and spun round, expecting to see the monster.

240

"Aaron!" I cried. I swallowed hard, trying to force down my fear. "Where—?"

"I waited for you," he said. His voice trembled. His hands were knotted into fists. He looked about ready to burst into tears.

"Aaron—"

"I've been waiting all this time," he said shrilly. "Where've you been? I've been so scared."

"I was . . . back there," I told him.

"I was ready to call the police or something," Aaron said. "I was hiding down the road. I—"

"You saw him?" I asked eagerly, suddenly remembering why we had risked our lives tonight. "You saw Mr Mortman?"

Aaron shook his head. "No, I didn't. I was too far away."

"But earlier," I said. "Through the window. When he was a monster. Didn't you see him then? Didn't you see him eat the snails and the eels?"

Aaron shook his head again. "I didn't see anything, Lucy," he said softly. "I'm sorry. I wish I had."

Big help, I thought bitterly.

Now what was I going to do?

"Mum—you don't understand. I *can't* go!"

"Lucy, I'm not giving you a choice. You're going, and that's that."

It was the next afternoon, a stormy, grey day, and Mum and I were in the kitchen, arguing. I was trying to tell her there was no way I could go to my Reading Rangers meeting at the library. And she was insisting that I had to go.

"Mum, you've got to believe me," I pleaded. I was trying not to whine, but my voice kept creeping higher and higher. "Mr Mortman is a monster. I can't go to the library any more."

Mum made a disgusted face and threw down the teatowel she'd been folding. "Lucy, your father and I have had it up to here with your silly monster stories."

She turned to face me. Her expression was angry. "The fact is, Lucy dear, that you are lazy. You never stick with anything. You're really lazy. That's your problem."

242

"Mr Mortman is a monster," I interrupted. "*That's* my problem."

"Well, I don't care," Mum replied sharply. "I don't care if he turns into a drooling werewolf at night. You're not giving up Reading Rangers. You're going to your appointment this afternoon if I have to take you by the hand and walk you there myself."

"Really—would you?" I asked.

The idea flashed into my head that Mum could hide in the stacks and see for herself when Mr Mortman turned into a monster.

But I think she thought I was being sarcastic. She just scowled and walked out of the kitchen.

And so, an hour later, I was trudging up the stone steps to the old library. It was raining hard, but I didn't take an umbrella. I didn't care if I got drenched.

My hair was soaked and matted on my head. I shook my head hard as I stepped into the entrance, sending drops of water flying in all directions.

I shivered, more from my fear, from being back in this frightening place, than from the cold. I pulled off my rucksack. It was dripping wet, too.

How can I face Mr Mortman? I wondered as I made my way reluctantly into the main reading room. How can I face him after last night?

He must surely suspect that I know his secret.

He *couldn't* have believed me last night, could he?

I was so furious with my mum for forcing me to come here.

I hope he turns into a monster and chews me to bits! I thought bitterly. That will really teach Mum a lesson.

I pictured Mum and Dad and Randy, sitting mournfully in our living room, crying their eyes out, wailing. "If only we had believed her! If only we had listened!"

Holding my wet rucksack in front of me like a shield, I made my way slowly past the long rows of books to the front of the room.

To my relief, there were several people in the library. I saw two little kids with their mothers and a couple of other women browsing in the mystery book section.

Great! I thought, starting to feel slightly calmer. Mr Mortman won't dare do anything while the library is filled with people.

The librarian was dressed in a green poloneck today, which really made him look like a big, round turtle. He was stamping a pile of books and didn't look up as I stepped close to the desk.

I cleared my throat nervously. "Mr Mortman?"

It took him a long while to look up. When he finally did, a warm smile formed above his chins. "Hi, Lucy. Give me a few minutes, okay?"

"Okay," I said. "I'll go and dry off."

He seems very friendly, I thought, heading over to a chair at one of the long tables. He doesn't seem angry at all.

Maybe he really did believe my story last night.

Maybe he really doesn't know that I've seen him turn into a monster.

Maybe I'll get out of here alive. . . .

I sat down at the table and shook some more water from my hair. I stared at the big, round wall clock, nervously waiting for him to call me up for our meeting. The clock ticked noisily. Each second seemed to take a minute.

The kids with their mothers checked out some books and left. I turned to the mystery section and saw that the two women had also cleared out. The librarian and I were the only ones left.

Mr Mortman shoved a pile of books across his desk and stood up. "I'll be right back, Lucy," he said, another friendly, reassuring smile on his face. "Then we'll have our meeting."

He stepped away from his desk and, walking briskly, headed for the back of the reading room. I supposed he was going to the toilet or something.

A jagged flash of white lightning flickered across the dark sky outside the window. It was followed by a drumroll of thunder.

I stood up from the table and, carrying my wet

rucksack by the straps, started towards Mr Mortman's desk.

I was halfway to the desk when I heard the loud click.

I knew at once that he had locked the front door.

A few seconds later, he returned, walking briskly, still smiling. He was rubbing his pudgy white hands together as he walked.

"Shall we talk about your book?" he asked, stepping up to me.

"Mr Mortman—you've locked the front door," I said, swallowing hard.

His smile didn't fade.

His dark little eyes locked on mine.

"Yes. Of course," he said softly, studying my face. His hands were still clasped together in front of him.

"But—why?" I stammered.

He brought his face close to mine, and his smile faded. "I know why you were at my house last night," he growled into my ear. "I know everything."

"But, Mr Mortman, I—"

"I'm sorry," he said in his throaty growl. "But I can't let you leave, Lucy. I can't let you leave the library."

"Ohhh." The sound escaped my lips, a moan of total terror.

I stared at him without moving. I suppose I wanted to see if he was serious or not. If he really meant what he said.

His eyes told me he did.

And as I stared at him, his head began to inflate. His tiny, round eyes shot out of their sockets and grew into throbbing, black bulbs.

"Ohhh."

Again, the terrified sound escaped my lips. My whole body convulsed in a shudder of terror.

His head was throbbing now, throbbing like a heart. His mouth opened into a gaping, gruesome leer, and green spittle ran down his quivering chin.

Move! I told myself. *Move, Lucy! DO something!*

His disgusting grin grew wider. His enormous head bobbed and throbbed excitedly.

He uttered a low growl of attack. And reached out both arms to grab me.

"No!" I shrieked.

I leaned back and, with all my might, swung the rucksack into his flabby stomach.

It caught him by surprise.

He gasped as it took his breath away.

I let go of the rucksack, spun round, and started to run.

He was right behind me. I could hear his panting breath and low, menacing growls.

I ran through a narrow aisle between two tall shelves.

A rumble of thunder from outside seemed to shake the room.

He was still behind me. Close. Closer.

He was going to catch me, going to grab me from behind.

I reached the end of the row. I hesitated. I didn't know which way to turn. I couldn't think.

He roared, a monstrous animal sound.

I turned left and started to run along the back wall of the room.

Another rumble of thunder.

"Ohh!" I realized to my horror that I'd made a mistake.

A fatal mistake.

I was running right into the corner.

There was no exit here. No escape.

He roared again, so loud that it drowned out the thunder.

I was trapped.

I knew it.

Trapped.

With a desperate cry, I ran blindly—headlong into the card catalogue.

Behind me, I heard the monster's roar of laughter.

He knew he had won.

The card catalogue toppled over. Drawers came sliding out. Cards spilled at my feet, scattering over the floor.

"Noooo!" the monster howled. At first I thought it was a victory cry. But then I realized it was an angry cry of protest.

With a moan of horror, he stooped to the floor and began gathering up the cards.

Staring in disbelief, I plunged past him, running frantically, my arms thrashing wildly at my sides.

In that moment of terror, I remembered the one thing that librarians hate most: having cards from the card catalogue spilled on the floor!

Mr Mortman was a monster—but he was also a librarian.

He couldn't bear to have those cards in disorder. He had to try to replace them before chasing after me.

It took only a few seconds to run into the front entrance, turn the lock, pull open the door, and flee out into the rain.

My trainers slapped the pavement as I ran, sending up splashes of rainwater.

I made my way to the street and was halfway up the block when I realized he was chasing after me.

A flash of lightning crackled to my left.

I cried out, startled, as a deafening burst of thunder shook the ground.

I glanced back to see how close the monster was.

And stopped.

With trembling hands, I frantically brushed a glaze of rainwater from my eyes.

"Aaron!" I cried. "What are *you* doing here?"

He ran up to me, hunching against the cold rain. He was breathing hard. His eyes were wide and frightened. "I—I was in the library," he stammered, struggling to catch his breath. "Hiding. I saw it. I saw the monster. I saw everything."

"You *did*?" I was so happy. I wanted to hug him.

A sheet of rain swept over us, driven by a gust of wind.

"Let's get to my house!" I cried. "You can tell my parents. Now maybe they'll finally believe it!"

251

Aaron and I burst into the study. Mum looked up from the sofa, lowering the newspaper to her lap. "You're dripping on the rug," she said.

"Where's Dad? Is he home yet?" I asked, rainwater running down my forehead. Aaron and I were soaked from head to foot.

"Here I am." He appeared behind us. He had changed out of his work clothes. "What's all the excitement?"

"It's about the monster!" I blurted out. "Mr Mortman—he—"

Mum shook her head and started to raise a hand to stop me.

But Aaron quickly came to my rescue. "I saw him, too!" Aaron exclaimed. "Lucy didn't make it up. It's true!"

Mum and Dad listened to Aaron. I knew they would.

He told them what he had seen in the library. He told them how the librarian had turned into a monster and chased me into the corner.

Mum listened intently to Aaron's story, shaking her head. "I suppose Lucy's story is true," she said when Aaron had finished.

"Yeah, I suppose it is," Dad said, putting a hand gently on my shoulder.

"Well, now that you *finally* believe me—what are you going to do, Dad?" I demanded.

He gazed at me thoughtfully. "We'll invite Mr Mortman to dinner," he said.

"Huh?" I goggled at him, rainwater running down my face. "You'll *what*? He tried to gobble me up! You *can't* invite him here!" I protested. "You can't!"

"Lucy, we have no choice," Dad insisted. "We'll invite him to dinner."

Mr Mortman arrived a few evenings later, carrying a bouquet of flowers. He was wearing lime-green trousers and a bright yellow, short-sleeved sports shirt.

Mum accepted the flowers from him and led him into the living room where Dad, Randy, and I were waiting. I gripped the back of a chair tightly as he entered. My legs felt rubbery, and my stomach felt as if I'd swallowed a heavy rock.

I *still* couldn't believe that Dad had invited Mr Mortman into our house!

Dad stepped forward to shake hands with the librarian. "We've been meaning to invite you for quite a while," Dad told him, smiling. "We want to thank you for the excellent reading course at the library."

"Yes," Mum joined in. "It's really meant a lot to Lucy."

Mr Mortman glanced at me uncertainly. I

254

could see that he was studying my expression. "I'm glad," he said, forcing a tight-lipped smile.

Mr Mortman lowered himself onto the sofa. Mum offered him a tray of crackers with cheese on them. He took one and chewed on it delicately.

Randy sat down on the rug. I was still standing behind the armchair, gripping the back of it so tightly, my hands ached. I had never been so nervous in all my life.

Mr Mortman seemed nervous, too. When Dad handed him a glass of iced tea, Mr Mortman spilled a little on his trousers. "It's such a humid day," he said. "This iced tea hits the spot."

"Being a librarian must be interesting work," Mum said, taking a seat beside Mr Mortman on the sofa.

Dad was standing at the side of the sofa.

They chatted for a while. As they talked, Mr Mortman kept darting glances at me. Randy, sitting cross-legged on the floor, drummed his fingers on the carpet.

Mum and Dad seemed calm and perfectly at ease. Mr Mortman seemed a little uncomfortable. He had glistening beads of perspiration on his shiny, round forehead.

My stomach growled loudly, more from nervousness than from hunger. No one seemed to hear it.

The three adults chatted for a while longer. Mr Mortman sipped his iced tea.

He leaned back on the sofa and smiled at my mother. "It was so kind of you to invite me. I don't get very many home-cooked meals. What's for dinner?" he asked.

"*You* are!" my Dad told him, stepping in front of the sofa.

"What?" Mr Mortman raised a hand behind his ear. "I didn't hear you correctly. What is for dinner?"

"*You* are!" Dad repeated.

"Ulllp!" Mr Mortman let out a little cry and turned bright red. He struggled to raise himself from the low sofa.

But Mum and Dad were too fast for him.

They both pounced on him. Their fangs popped down. And they gobbled the librarian up in less than a minute, bones and all.

Randy laughed gleefully.

I had a big smile on my face.

My brother and I haven't got our fangs yet. That's why we couldn't join in.

"Well, that's that," Mum said, standing up and straightening the sofa cushion. Then she turned to Randy and me. "That's the first monster to come to Timberland Falls in nearly twenty years," she told us. "That's why it took us so long to believe you, Lucy."

"You certainly gobbled him up fast!" I exclaimed.

"In a few years, you'll get your fangs," Mum said.

"Me, too!" Randy declared. "Then maybe I won't be afraid of monsters any more!"

Mum and Dad chuckled. Then Mum's expression turned serious. "You both understand why we had to do that, don't you? We can't allow any *other* monsters in town. It would frighten the whole community. And we don't *want* people to get frightened and chase us away. We like it here!"

Dad burped loudly. "Pardon me," he said, covering his mouth

Later that night, I was upstairs in Randy's room. He was all tucked in, and I was telling him a bedtime story.

". . . And so the librarian hid behind the tall bookshelf," I said in a low, whispery voice. "And when the little boy named Randy reached up to pull a book down from the shelf, the librarian stuck his long arms through the shelf and *grabbed* the boy, and—"

"Lucy, how many times do I have to tell you?"

I glanced up to see Mum standing in the doorway, a frown on her face.

"I don't want you frightening your little brother before bedtime," Mum scolded. "You'll give him nightmares. Now, come on, Lucy—no more monster stories!"

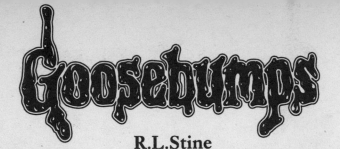

Goosebumps

R.L. Stine

Reader beware, you're in for a scare!
These terrifying tales will send shivers up your spine:

Goosebumps

Reader beware – you choose the scare!

Give Yourself Goosebumps

A scary new series from R.L. Stine – where
you decide what happens!

Choose from over 20 scary endings!

GOOSEBUMPS

Reader beware — here's THREE TIMES the scare!

Look out for these bumper GOOSEBUMPS editions. With three spine-tingling stories by R.L. Stine in each book, get ready for three times the thrill … three times the scare … three times the GOOSEBUMPS!

COLLECTION 1
Welcome to Dead House
Say Cheese and Die
Stay Out of the Basement

COLLECTION 2
The Curse of the Mummy's Tomb
Let's Get Invisible!
Night of the Living Dummy

COLLECTION 3
The Girl Who Cried Monster
Welcome to Camp Nightmare
The Ghost Next Door

COLLECTION 4
The Haunted Mask
Piano Lessons Can Be Murder
Be Careful What You Wish For

COLLECTION 5
The Werewolf of Fever Swamp
You Can't Scare Me!
One Day at HorrorLand

COLLECTION 6
Why I'm Afraid of Bees
Deep Trouble
Go Eat Worms

COLLECTION 7
Return of the Mummy
The Scarecrow Walks at Midnight
Attack of the Mutant

HIPPO GHOST

Summer Visitors

Emma thinks she's in for a really boring summer,
until she meets the Carstairs family on the beach.
But there's something very *strange* about her
new friends. . .

Carol Barton

Ghostly Music

Beth loves her piano lessons. So why have they
started to make her *ill*. . . ?

Richard Brown

A Patchwork of Ghosts

Who is the evil-looking ghost tormenting Lizzie,
and why does he want to hurt her...?

Angela Bull

The Ghosts who Waited

Everything's changed since Rosy and her family
moved house. Why has everyone suddenly
turned against her. . .?

Dennis Hamley

The Railway Phantoms

Rachel has visions. She dreams of two children
in strange, disintegrating clothes. And it seems
as if they are trying to contact her...

Dennis Hamley

The Haunting of Gull Cottage

Unless Kezzie and James can find what really
happened in Gull Cottage that terrible night
many years ago, the haunting may never stop...
Tessa Krailing

The Hidden Tomb

Can Kate unlock the mystery of the curse on
Middleton Hall, before it destroys the Mason
family...?
Jenny Oldfield

The House at the End of Ferry Road

The house at the end of Ferry Road has just
been built. So it can't be haunted, can it...?
Martin Oliver

Beware! This House is Haunted
This House is Haunted Too!

Jessica doesn't believe in ghosts. So who *is*
writing the strange, spooky messages?
Lance Salway

The Children Next Door

Laura longs to make friends with the children
next door. But they're not quite what they seem...
Jean Ure